THE MEAT HOOK KILLER

A chilling crime thriller with a stunning final twist

EMMY ELLIS

DI Bethany Smith Book 7

Originally published as *Evil is the Butcher*

JOFFE BOOKS

Revised edition 2023
Joffe Books, London
www.joffebooks.com

First published in Great Britain in 2020
as *Evil is the Butcher*

This paperback edition was first published
in Great Britain in 2023

Cover art by Dee Dee Book Covers

ISBN: 978-1-83526-163-7

PROLOGUE

The hook. The smell. The feel.
Revolting. Beautiful. Safe.

That stench he hated yet loved wafted. Strange to be so contrary, considering, but there it was. You couldn't change how you felt. Or maybe you could. The thing was, Roland didn't want to. Not now. It was all too late for turning over that new leaf people kept banging on about. He was forty-three, for fuck's sake.

No. He wouldn't change.

He sniffed, smiling. How was it that a dead body could incite such pleasure? Most people would shit a brick and recoil, but Roland, he loved it.

The fresher the better.

He giggled at that. This one was fresh, buried so recently. Except she wasn't in her coffin anymore. Angela Lockwood, her grave marker said. *May you rest in eternal peace, beautiful lady.* Well, she wasn't exactly resting, not while she hung off the butcher's hook in the back of his artic lorry. It was one of those massive buggers, big enough for him to park his little car inside. He needed the Fiat for his trips. Inconspicuous. Him haring round in the artic would get noticed, so he'd be stupid to try it.

And that was one thing he wasn't, stupid.

He climbed on his stepladder, leant forward, and gave Angela's cheek a long lick, tasting her deadness, her skin spongy beneath his eager tongue. He needed this, the flavour, the scent of the unliving snaking up his nostrils.

Yes, he needed this Angela woman.

She'd look so good once she'd rotted. Shrivelled. Dried out. A different taste altogether then, and her odour would be like nothing else as she decomposed. It'd filter into the cab, keeping him company while he drove, a miasmic passenger.

He could hardly wait.

"Who were you?" he shouted. God, he sounded so manly it was unreal. He needed to be a man, his daddy had told him that. "Who have you left behind, you fucking bitch?"

And she had to be a bitch. All women were. At least those who walked out on their children. Yet Angela's marker had said she was a beautiful lady, so that confused him.

He gritted his teeth, shuddering at the thought of having made a mistake. What if this woman had loved her kids, had never left their side? What if she was nothing like his mother?

No. He wouldn't entertain that. It suited his purposes for her to be a cow.

"You let men mess about with you," he whispered. "You let them touch your body, you dirty thing. They licked you. Like I did."

He slid his tongue up her cheek again, halting just beneath her eye. The lashes tickled, and his 'maggot' tickled, too. Daddy called it that. A maggot.

"It's nothing but useless like this, boy," he'd said. "Can't do much with that, can we? Here, I'll make it grow . . ."

Roland turned away from Angela and closed his eyes. Breathed deeply. Thought about when he'd taken her from her wooden box, the effort of digging up all that mud. It hadn't had a chance to compact, so it could have been a harder job, and he didn't have grass to get rid of, her grave being so new.

Small mercies.

He climbed down the ladder and spun to face her. "Mummy, will you give me a cuddle?"

Roland pressed himself to Angela, curling his arms around her, his cheek flush to her pelvis. She hung high, as did the others, and he stepped back, releasing her. He adored watching them swing. It was like they came alive again.

"That's it. You dance for your little lad," he said.

Angela's hair, so perfect since he'd brushed it, wavered with her movement. It was as though a summer breeze soughed through the lorry, tweaking each strand. But she didn't look right. Not yet.

He walked to his Fiat and got inside, taking a packet of large white stickers from the glove box. He drew a smiling mouth, the red of the thick marker just like Mum's lipstick, the kind she put on when she'd gone to meet those men Daddy had told him all about. Back in front of Angela, he stuck the lips on hers. They matched the sticker on his mouth. And there she was, a good mother, a kind mother, nothing like the one who'd left him.

Here, when he wasn't thinking of her as a bitch, he could dream. Pretend. She was decent and loved him. While she didn't smell of her sweet perfume, that didn't matter. What did was that she was here, with him. They all were.

Angela stopped swaying, so he moved to Jen Ferguson, the one he'd dug up before Angela. Last month, it was, down in Cheshire. He travelled the roads in search of places that felt right and stayed for long enough to find a butcher, kill him, and dispose of him in a new grave.

He needed their testicles to become more manly.

"You're a good girl," he told Jen. "You've loved staying here with me, haven't you?" He licked her to test whether she tasted different to yesterday, and she did, more dead, more delicious. He curled a lock of her hair around his mud-stained finger.

She smiled her red sticker smile.

And he smiled his.

CHAPTER ONE

Owen cringed. Dave, his boss, laughed at something a customer had said in answer to his question, a stupid joke that was by no means funny. Like they hadn't heard it a million and one times before.

Ooh, having a bit of meat tonight, are you, madam?

Yes, Dave, I love a sausage.

Owen didn't think he could stand it for the rest of his working life, that sort of inane chatter, but a job was a job, and being a butcher's apprentice wasn't to be sniffed at, not when lads his age struggled to find work. With him having well low GCSE grades because he'd fucked about at school, employers hadn't looked at him, let alone given an interview. Except for Dave, that was. He'd taken a chance, said you didn't have to have good exam results to learn how to cut meat, and he'd be a pro in no time, just you wait and see.

"Did you hear that, Givens?" Dave asked him, his cheeks rosy, like he'd downed one too many whiskies in an overly warm pub.

Owen held back a sigh and switched off the mincemeat machine, annoyed, yet again, at the way Dave always called him by his surname. "What's that then?"

"A good worker, him," Dave said to the customer. He winked and nodded, sagely, as some of the old grannies liked so say. "So engrossed in mincing, he didn't get the pleasure of listening to your joke."

Oh, I did. I fucking well did. Owen smiled, the outside of him presenting as happy, but inside he was tired. "Sorry, I was miles away."

"Tell it again, Marlene." Dave gestured as if winding up that gramophone he'd found recently in the charity shop, a right old bargain at a fiver.

Marlene, a regular who came in every Wednesday without fail — unless you counted that time she'd had a dodgy stomach from the shellfish she'd bought up the road, or when she went on holiday — gave a creamy-denture smile and tittered. Owen reckoned she fancied Dave, even though he must be thirty years her junior. She was always fluttering her eyelashes at him or pouting in what she must have thought was a sexy way.

Owen shuddered.

"Oh, okay then." Marlene grinned.

She flattened a skinny hand on her chest, the veins prominent, turquoise bulging rivers across a wrinkled brown landscape. She'd recently been to Tenerife, hence the tan, and they'd endured numerous stories over the past week of what she'd got up to there. Apparently, she'd copped off with a Spanish waiter — "In his twenties, he was, and a right goer!" — but Owen didn't believe a word of it. Who'd want to shag an old lady? He certainly wouldn't, and he was twenty-one.

Marlene cleared her throat and glanced between them. "Well, I want some chicken — for a casserole, you know — and told Dave I'm hoping for the *breast* in what he selects for me, instead of the *worst*."

Owen did his duty and roared, a bit too enthusiastically mind you, but Dave and Marlene didn't seem to notice.

"Breast. Good one." *Better than the crap about sausages at any rate.*

She laughed, all ancient woman and raspy — fifty fags a day, that one — and kept her beady eye on Dave, who picked up said breast and slapped it on the weighing machine in a white plastic bag with DAVE JOHNSON, BUTCHER on the front in red, the face of a cartoon pig beneath.

"Three seventy-five," Dave said, "but you can have it for two-fifty with another boob thrown in."

"Boob!" She squealed, and her dentures almost shot out she was that manic. She stuffed them back in place, and they clattered together.

Owen shuddered again at the thought of those teeth coming loose when she was with the Spaniard. Christ, he'd had enough. It was only Wednesday, and the week already seemed long — too long, what with the customers intent on stocking up because that storm was on its way. He supposed they didn't want to get caught out with no meat in, but God, it wasn't the apocalypse, was it. The damn thing was only predicted to last a day, and him and Dave would be coming to work, as usual, Dave saying no bit of rain and wind would keep him away. The inevitable joke about bodily gases had followed — wind — and really, Owen had wanted to cry. Dad jokes got so old when you heard them too often.

Marlene took her 'boobs' off the counter and placed them in her pull-along polka-dot shopping trolley — pink background, white spots, and the handle had one of those bright-orange rubber things on it, so she'd have a better grip, she'd said during one of her monotonous tales. She paid Dave, her hand shaking as she ferreted in her leather purse.

"I bought this purse in Tenerife, a bargain for a tenner, and my neighbour wants one, but that's just tough because I'll not buy her one when I go back. Besides, I don't think the woman deserves it because she's always shitting in the communal bathroom at the sheltered housing instead of using her own. The damn thing doesn't flush properly, and 'remnants' are left behind."

Remnants . . .

She went on about having to cook chasseur for her daughter and grandchildren when they came round later, and oh, she must nip to the greengrocer's and pick up some mushrooms for that. You can't have a chasseur without those, apparently.

Fuck me sideways . . .

Owen tuned her out, stabbing the ON button for the mincer, thinking of his date tonight with Charlotte Howard, that saucy bint who came in every Monday morning to collect steak for her dog. They were going to the Flapping Crow for pub grub, nothing fancy, as his wage packet didn't stretch that far, but it'd be nice to have a sit down and a natter, get to know her more. They'd met up twice before and got along well, and you never knew, did you, whether it could turn into something serious.

"Can you attend to this gentleman, Givens?" Dave asked.

Owen all but punched the OFF button. How was he meant to get all the meat done if he kept being interrupted? He swivelled and smiled, then had to fix that grin in place once he clapped eyes on who wanted serving. It was that creepy bloke, the one with sore skin all around his mouth, like he'd had something stuck there, and when he'd taken it off, it'd ripped the top layer away.

"How can I help you?" Owen asked, his voice weak, and he hated it that this fella always reduced him to feeling small. He'd secretly named him Willy Weirdo and had slipped up once during a convo with Dave and received a *tsk* for his trouble.

Dave bustled off out the back, probably to use the loo, and Owen maintained his smile, despite coming over all odd — sticky skin, shivers up his spine, the hairs on the back of his neck rising.

Willy Weirdo stared, as he always did. Every bloody day he was in here this past month, his excuse being that he didn't have much space in the small freezer compartment inside his fridge, so fresh was best. And he always said that each time an' all.

"A ribeye, please, the bloodier the better." Willy's shaved head had little black dots all over it where new hair growth was coming through. "And make it a big fat one. I do like a slab of flesh."

Owen opted for the thickest one on the tray and held it up for him to see. Blood dripped off it.

Willy nodded. "That'll do, Donkey. Seen *Shrek*, have you?"

"Yes." Owen nodded.

"Ah, but have you ever eaten testicles?"

Owen dropped the meat on the weighing scales, sure he hadn't heard him right. The swift change of topic was so sodding *strange*. "Um, sorry?"

"Testicles. Ever eaten them?"

"Can't say I have." Owen pressed the button that ensured a price sticker chuntered out of the side of the scales. "Seen it on *I'm a Celebrity*, though. People eating them, I mean, in the Bushtucker Trials."

"They're a bit dry but a necessity if you want to be manly."

"Right . . ." Owen folded the bag over and secured it with the price sticker. He glanced to his left in the hopes he'd see Dave. Nope. "Can I get you anything else?"

"No. I've told you before, I need to buy daily. Fresh is best."

Owen didn't roll his eyes, but bloody hell, he wanted to. Maybe he ought to go to college in the evenings, study to resit his exams. He'd get a better job without having to deal with dickheads like this one then. No Marlene and her lies about Spanish men. No Mrs Simmons with the cauliflower ear, an injury from her former husband who liked to clout it on as many occasions as possible. No Katherine Willows, who left her barking mutt outside, one of those huge bastards, a Malumite or something. Malamute, that was it. He'd never been much cop at remembering breeds.

"Yes, fresh is best," Owen parroted.

"You're a bit . . ." Willy leant forward. "A bit wimpy, aren't you?"

All right, Owen wasn't the beefiest, but he wasn't a wimp. He did judo. "I don't know what you mean, sir." He rested the steak bag on the glass counter.

"Get a few testicles," Willy said. "Fry them up with a bit of garlic. Then you'll be a man's man with some balls in you."

Owen didn't want to eat testicles, and he didn't want to stand here talking to this fucker either, but he had no choice until Dave came back. What was he doing, having a shit? It seemed like he'd been gone ages.

"Okay, I'll do that." Owen smiled, even though it didn't sit right.

"See that you do." Willy handed over a tenner. "Oh, and if you season that mince with pepper, it makes for a tastier chilli or whatever."

"I'll pass that info on to Dave. Thanks." Owen rung the purchase up on the till and handed back the change. Four pounds and five pence.

"You can't skimp on steak." Willy took the money. "Better from a human, but a cow will have to do."

Owen jolted at that. What the hell was wrong with this freak?

"Joke." The steak bag disappeared into the pocket of Willy's grey puffa. "See you."

Owen said goodbye, relieved he didn't have to deal with him anymore. The woof of Katherine Willows' dog brought his attention to the window, and she chained him up on the post beside the outdoor fridge display, right next to the pre-packed burgers and sausages, for God's sake. One of these days that mutt was going to nick a packet and eat them, and Katherine would moan about having to pay for it.

Dave breezed in, appearing a lot more harried than he had when he'd left, muttering something about "that bloody supplier", but he took over serving Katherine, and Owen went back to the mincer, grinding his teeth along with the beef at the dog's noise, wishing he was anywhere but here.

Only four hours left to go.

* * *

Dave had let Givens go home half an hour early, what with the lad having a date, plus Dave had received a worrying phone call earlier from the meat supplier — something about the pork not being ready yet. Besides that, the rain had started, and a fair old wind had picked up, whooshing beneath the red-and-white-striped awning and pushing it upwards, creating a ship's sail. The bloody thing would take off if he wasn't careful, so he stepped outside and wound the canopy in. Givens had already brought the packaged meat in, plus wheeled the outdoor fridge round the back and into the covered yard, so all Dave had left to do was clean the last two steel trays in the glass counter.

The high street was empty.

He closed the front door and drew the blinds over it and the window. No sense staying open if no one was about. He got to work, packing away the minced beef, now seasoned with pepper, thanks to Givens suggesting it. It wasn't a bad idea at all, and in future, he'd get the kid to do half and half whenever he did that job. Best to have a choice. Some people didn't like pepper, did they.

A clatter came from the yard, and he frowned. Givens had closed the gate, but it wasn't locked until Dave went upstairs to his flat. Maybe some kids had got in, playing hide and seek or whatever. He'd give them what for and send them on their way, the little blighters.

He jogged out the back and into the yard, but the gate was shut, and no kids fucked about. He walked around, checking beneath the fridge under its tarpaulin cover, then went back inside and nosed in his breeze-block carcase room to make sure no one had come in to steal a cow, pig, or sheep.

The dead animals hung from their hooks as they always did, except one swung slightly, and that wasn't right. Unless a heavy hook had somehow fallen . . . But they weren't weighty enough to move a whole cow.

Hmm.

He weaved between each carcase, frowning some more, puzzled because there wasn't anyone here. Dave shrugged and left the room, closing the door, and entered the space behind the shop.

That man stood there, the customer who only had a little freezer compartment — he told Dave about it every day, as if it was important to him. What was it Givens had called him? Willy Weirdo, that was it. Dave had told him off for it, but now he could see what Givens meant. The bloke *was* strange, and he *did* give off a creepy air.

"Oh, came out here to find me, did you?" Dave asked, annoyed someone had gone around the counter into the private area. That wasn't on. "I could have sworn I heard your voice earlier, talking to Givens — you don't normally shop twice in one day. Maybe I imagined it."

Willy didn't move. He had his usual grey puffa jacket on but had a transparent plastic poncho over the top, the kind festivalgoers used to keep the rain off. The hood covered his bald head, and Dave supposed that was sensible, since the heavens had well and truly opened now, the eye of the storm on the way.

"Let's go out the front then, shall we?" Dave prompted. What he'd really wanted to say was: *Get the fuck out, you spooky bastard.* Not good for business, that, airing your personal feelings when it could lose you a sale.

"Daddy?" Willy tilted his head. "I need to be a man." He stuck his thumb in his mouth and sucked on it, saliva dribbling down his chin.

Well now, that was a tad odd, and Dave wasn't sure what to do. He was no match for the big bloke so couldn't manhandle him from the shop, but what else could he do? He was uncomfortable, too uncomfortable, and needed this fella gone.

"I've got some cracking steaks left if you want another one. On the house, because I'm just about to close up."

Willy raised his free arm. "Cuddle me, Daddy," he muttered around the thumb.

Dave shivered, couldn't disguise it either, and took a step forward to go around Willy. If he could just get into the shop proper, he could use the phone if he had to. But was ringing the police warranted? Willy hadn't done anything except say iffy things, but he reckoned trespassing might get the coppers here.

"That steak then." Dave smiled and took another step forward.

Willy flung his arm out, barring Dave's way, and snatched his thumb out of his mouth. "I need your testicles."

Dave's heart went crackers, and his knees turned wobbly. "Wh . . . what? We don't sell those."

"Yours." Willy gripped Dave around the throat, lifting him off the floor.

Dave kicked him, but it didn't have any effect. He struggled to be free, to breathe, his cheeks heating, the skin there and on his forehead straining from the pressure. Dave summoned all his strength and raised his arms to punch the man, but after a couple of strikes to his chest, his energy decreased.

He could actually *feel* the life draining out of him, the burn of his lungs sharp then dull, his head going fuzzy.

"That's it, Daddy. Sleep now."

Dave closed his eyes. This was it, the end, and there wasn't a damn thing he could do about it.

CHAPTER TWO

Roland smiled at Daddy Dave, who was dead on the meat-cutting slab, in pieces, chopped up expertly like he'd been taught. It was so much easier to transport them this way, and using the butcher's shop meant he could clean up with the hose as if nothing was amiss.

He had the testicles. He'd cook them later in the little kitchenette in the back of the artic, and all the mums would watch, telling him he was a good and clever boy, knowing how to use the gas ring.

He wondered whether Angela had settled in with the others now they'd had a chance to chat without him listening. Sometimes it was preferable to talk without your son there, more private, and she could open up better.

He washed his gloves then popped each body part into double-strength black bags — he'd learnt the hard way at first, putting too much in, the bags breaking, blood leaking. While he didn't hang around for long after he'd killed the butchers, he couldn't risk being caught. Mummy wouldn't be proud of him if that happened.

The testicles he popped in one of the butcher's little meat bags, using a price sticker from the weighing scales to tape it up. He slid them in his jacket pocket, then carried the black bags out the back to his Fiat, which he'd brought into the yard once Dave Johnson had carked it.

The storm had darkened the sky more than it usually was at this time — seven o'clock on an autumn evening — and the road behind the shops didn't have any houses or whatnot on it. None close anyway. They were on the other side of some scrubland, too far for anyone to spot who he was. He was free as a bird to drive off.

He put his head down so the rain didn't get in his face, jogging across the yard to his car. The bags went in the boot, him taking a few trips back and forth, then he returned inside to clean up. By the time he'd finished, it was nine fifteen, and he got in the driver's seat that he'd covered in thick plastic.

The drive to the cemetery didn't take long, and he smiled at how he'd left the yard gates open, so, come the morning, someone would know Dave hadn't locked up. They'd look for him, think he'd just disappeared into thin air, and that would be that. He was surprised none of the daddies had made the news. All of them being butchers was surely a big clue. Them going missing was suspicious, but no one had picked up on that yet. Or if they had, they'd chosen not to use the media for an appeal.

He parked behind the groundsman's hut. The fucker finished work at five and secured both sets of iron gates with padlocks. The season meant earlier closing times. That didn't matter. Roland had already worked out what to do. Of course he had. He'd collected Angela last night so knew the score.

Using his bolt cutters, he broke the padlock and slipped it into his pocket beside the other one he'd purchased. He'd bought the one on the gate, too, which had annoyingly only come with one key. Had the groundsman noticed? Wondered why a key had dangled from it?

What did it bloody matter anyway?

He opened the gate and carried the black bags through to Angela's grave, going from memory in the dark, again making a few trips. Then he locked himself in with the new padlock and stood next to her grave marker, bending to stroke the top.

"Daddy will take your place now, Mummy, like he always should have. He belongs here, not you."

It took a while to dig the mud with his large-ended shovel, the sky blackening further so he was working blind. And the weather didn't help, the wind battering him, shoving him to one side. He didn't go down as deep as he had when getting Mummy out. All he needed was enough depth to conceal the bags, and by next week, turf would be laid, the groundsman thinking the earth had had enough time to settle. Only once it sank would the old fella realise something was wrong, and by then, Roland would be long gone.

He dropped the bags inside in a line, each one thudding wetly on the rain-drenched mud. Once, he'd put them in the empty coffin, but it had taken too much time, and he'd slipped while climbing out of the hole using his rope ladder secured above with hooks that dug into the ground. You learnt as you went along, that was what he told himself, and why waste effort when you didn't need to?

Putting the mud back was an arduous task. Too much rain. Too much wind. His face stung, especially around his mouth where the sticker lips had been pressed. Still, he carried on until the bags were covered, and he'd just have to hope the remaining nodules of mud beside the grave didn't raise any red flags — maybe the rain would sort that. All the other times had been dry, and he'd used his handheld hoover to suck up all the bits, leaving the sites as clean as they'd been before he'd interfered with them.

He stood at the end, head bowed, and recited a prayer.

"Dearly beloved, we are gathered here today to lay to rest a bastard, one who didn't deserve to live. Daddy was a bad man, chasing Mummy away, preying on his son in dreadful ways . . . so very dreadful. God, please refuse him entry and send him to Hell where he belongs. Daddy is minus his balls, as is only right, as he taunted his son's lack of them enough, so it's only fitting he hasn't got any now. Daddy, I hope you burn in the flames. Amen."

He picked up his shovel and perched it on his shoulder for the trek back to his car, staggering every so often from the buffeting wind. It was so strong, an unseen sheet that pushed him, doing a good job of preventing him from leaving. He pressed ahead until he reached the gate, then secured it, dropping the shovel in the boot and diving into the driver's seat, out of the harsh elements.

The poncho was clean of Daddy's blood, the deluge sluicing it all away. He lowered the hood, and some water drizzled down his neck. He shivered at the coldness, starting the engine and turning the heater to maximum. He was soon toasty and patted his pocket, the testicles a comfort beneath his palm.

Later, he'd eat them.

That'd be nice.

* * *

Owen had come back to work, hoping Dave was awake upstairs in his flat so Owen could pick up his phone. He'd been out with Charlotte already — she'd left early as she needed a full night's sleep for work tomorrow — and she'd asked him why he hadn't responded to her message prior to them meeting up. That was when he'd twigged he didn't have his mobile, and he needed it so he could read his Kindle app on it in bed. If he didn't do that, it'd take him ages to drop off, and with the wind howling, he'd have even less of a chance.

No lights shone from the flat windows, and he reckoned Dave must have gone to bed. He stood outside in the street, staring up. The curtains weren't drawn, which was odd, because Dave had said more than once he didn't like sitting there with them open. The gym opposite was on three storeys, and one was level with his living room. He didn't want nosy parkers gawping while they used the treadmill, sweating away, and he sat there sipping his hot chocolate. It'd put him off his drink.

Maybe he'd gone out.

Again, that was odd. The only place Dave went was the Flapping Crow up the road, and Owen had just come from there. No sign of Dave propping up the bar at all with his usual Guinness and packet of peanuts.

Owen moved forward. The blind was down on the front door, but there was a slice of glass visible at the edge. He peered in. At the back of the shop, a faint line of light escaped through the gap between the internal door and the frame. It led to the space beyond, where they cut up all the meat. Dave might be working late or something.

A stout gust of wind smacked into Owen from behind, sending him rushing forward. He raised his hands to brace himself on the door, but it gave way, and he tumbled inside, landing on his knees. Pain lanced up his thighs. Shit, this storm could go and do one. The damn thing had only just started, so God knew how bad it would be by tomorrow. Charlotte's brown hair had flown all over the place when they'd come out of the pub.

Owen got up, worried now. The front door shouldn't be open. There was no way Dave wouldn't have locked up, even if he *was* still working.

Something clattered, an irritating, steady smack, and it ramped up his unease. Owen rounded the counter and walked into the back space, but Dave wasn't standing at the steel table, hacking off a lamb's legs or slicing pork for chops. It was clean and tidy, but the hose hadn't been put away right. That was strange, too. Dave was a stickler for ensuring it was coiled around the plastic housing properly so it didn't kink. The hose was a jumble, and a figure of eight drooped down, touching the floor. Dave would have a right fit about that, so why had he done it?

"Dave?"

Owen's voice echoed back at him, along with the constant clattering, and he shivered, overcome with a terrible sense of foreboding. He checked inside the meat room, but everything was as it should be. Then he went out into the yard, scanning the area. The wooden gate crashed back and forth, the wind having a right old time of pushing it to and fro. Owen ran across, out from beneath the covering, instantly getting wet, jostled by the wind.

He managed to secure the gate and padlocked it, all the while wondering why Dave hadn't done it. His boss didn't run a car so wouldn't have gone for a ride. The only other place he could be was in the flat. He'd probably fallen asleep before he'd had a chance to shut the curtains.

Upstairs, he went into each room, switching the lights on. Dave wasn't in any of them, and no plate with a knife and fork sat in the washing-up bowl. Only his cup was there, perhaps from the coffee he'd had before work — always a latte, always from his pod machine. The gramophone had pride of place on the living room sideboard, a record by some ancient band on top.

Owen turned all the lights off and went back downstairs. This wasn't right, none of it, but he didn't know what to do. Lock up and come back tomorrow, bright and early? He spied his phone on the shelf in the meat-cutting area and grabbed it, prodding at the screen to call Dave. The ringing sounded in his ear and in the shop, so he went out there and found Dave's mobile beside the weighing scales.

Certain now that something was way off, Owen cut the call and phoned the police. He felt stupid as fuck telling the woman on the other end that his boss had left his shop open and wasn't around, but what else could he have done? Locking up and going home wasn't an option, not with Dave's phone right there. It was never far from him.

"Okay, sir," the woman said. "We'll send officers. Go outside, just in case someone's in there and you just didn't spot them."

That gave Owen the willies, so he rushed into the violent weather, getting soaked and swept sideways. He shut the front door and huddled in the little porchway, which sometimes served as a bedroom for the homeless. It afforded him some respite from the storm, so that was something.

It didn't take long, and a police car drove down the road and parked at the kerb. Two officers got out, minus their hats, and it was just as well. They'd have got blown off within seconds. They ran towards him and squeezed into the spaces beside him.

"I'm PC Glen Underby, and this is PC Tory Yates," the man said. "I understand you're worried about your boss."

Owen nodded and explained everything, crapping his pants at the thought that they might think he'd done something to Dave. Then he remembered he'd been with Charlotte, and loads of people would have seen him in the pub. He hadn't had *time* to do anything to Dave. Well, not as well as getting rid of him, too.

"All I know is, Dave wouldn't have left the shop door open, or the gate, and he most definitely wouldn't have put the hose away like that."

Underby nodded. "So that's what stood out to you the most?"

"Well, yes, because Dave would go mental about it. I always have to wind it round the holder properly." He didn't say: *Someone else must have done it.* He had nothing to base that on, only that Dave was missing. He couldn't go around accusing whoever of fucking up the hose, and who the hell would have wanted to use it anyway?

"We'll nip inside and have a look. You stay here," Underby said.

The coppers went inside, and Owen felt too alone, too exposed, even though people were working their knackers off in the gym. What if someone had robbed Dave and bundled him away? What if he was hurt somewhere?

The police came back, and relief sagged Owen's shoulders.

"Right, put a pair of these gloves on for me," Yates said, "because I need you to check the till. I have no clue how they work."

Owen followed them inside and opened the drawer. The takings were still in there, and that was *not* normal. "Dave wouldn't have left this cash in here. He always counts the takings at half five, then does the float, and he puts the till tray in the safe."

"Okay, do you know how to open the safe?" Underby asked.

"Dave keeps the key on him."

"Did you spot them when you walked around?"

"No."

Underby glanced at Yates then back to Owen. "What we're going to do is take your name, address, and phone number, then look into this. We'll get hold of you if we find out anything — I assume you're due into work in the morning."

Owen nodded.

"One more thing," Yates said. "Where were you this evening before coming here?"

So they *did* think he'd done something. Bloody hell! He'd never done a bad thing in his life. Not like this anyway. Yeah, he'd nicked a Lion bar from the corner shop once — felt guilty for weeks, had nightmares an' all, of the police coming to arrest him for it — but anything beyond the usual childhood crap, no way.

"In the Flapping Crow." He jerked his thumb in that direction. "With Charlotte Howard. Want her phone number as well?"

"That would be great," Yates said. "What time did you get there?"

He scratched his head. He knew the answer, but now she was asking, his brain played up on him. "Let me think a second. I left here at five — Dave let me go early. I went home in my car." He rattled off his address. "Then I came straight back to town after a shower. Had to meet Charlotte at quarter past six." He explained her early night. "But there was a stop light that wouldn't turn from red for ages, so I was stuck in traffic until about twenty-five past. When I finally got parked and in the pub, I was late, obviously, and

Charlotte had messaged me, asking where I was. Then I realised I didn't have my phone so came here after the date, which was about ten minutes before I called you lot."

"Okay, thank you." Yates smiled.

Uneasy that he appeared to be a suspect, Owen asked, "So I can go now?"

"You've given us your address. We just need your full name and phone number, plus Charlotte's."

Owen gave them, shaking. Christ, what must it be like if you'd really done something? He was worrying they'd pin it on him when he was innocent. He'd read about that kind of thing. "Look, this has nothing to do with me."

"We didn't say it did." Underby smiled, too.

It was a nice one, kind, and Owen relaxed a bit.

"All standard procedure," Underby said.

"Right." Owen swiped his palms down his thighs then stopped — they could think he was sweating buckets because he was scared of being caught for this . . . this whatever it was. "I'm off then."

"We'll be in touch for a proper statement," Yates informed him. "Or you can go into the station and give one in the morning."

"What about work, though?" Owen frowned.

"This may well be a crime scene," Yates said. "You might not be coming to work."

Owen shook his head. It was one thing to imagine something had happened, you know, think it to yourself, but to have someone else confirm your fears?

Fuck me . . .

He managed a wave and stumbled out of the shop, the wind propelling him to his car.

Where was Dave? And if he'd been kidnapped or something, where had he been taken?

CHAPTER THREE

Bethany laughed at Leona, who'd been telling them about the previous evening. She'd put homemade macaroni cheese into the oven and fallen asleep. By the time she'd woken, the top layer was black, and she could have used it for a chalk-board, so she'd said.

"So what did you end up eating?" Fran swivelled from side to side on her desk chair. It creaked, and she winced, stopping the motion.

"Same thing but from a tin." Leona shrugged.

"Eww." Tammy pulled a face. "You know the crap they put in that sort of stuff, don't you?"

Leona sniffed. "Better than going hungry. I was too groggy to give a monkey's chuff by then anyway. I stumbled to bed straight after, slept right through. I managed to make porridge okay this morning, though."

Bethany's phone rang, and she slid it out of her pocket, hoping it was a new case they could get their teeth into. Not that she wished anyone dead, of course not, but things had been quiet around here since the Tic Tac Toe saga, and they'd been looking into cold cases and smaller serious crimes, in particular, a man who kept beating his wife up every Friday after he'd chugged a few too many gins at the pub. He liked using his fists and made no bones about it when he was questioned.

The wife, Laura Tremmings, always called the police, hysterical and begging for help as if her old man had murder on his mind, but once that help arrived, she refused to press charges. It was at the point where the police were going to press them. Enough was enough. The man's behaviour couldn't be allowed to continue. Fran and Leona were going round to the address today to speak to Laura and explain what was going to happen — whether she liked it or not. Tammy was staying behind to sort the paperwork for the CPS.

"Hi," Bethany said. "What can I do for you, Rob?"

The daytime desk sergeant sighed. "A bit of a weird one for you."

"Ninety-five per cent of them are weird, but go on . . ."

"Okay. A grave has been disturbed, a recent one, and black bags were buried there. Thing is, the bags have body parts in them."

"Oh, bugger me," she said. "Have you done a check on missing persons, or am I being a div asking that? Of course you have."

He laughed. "I did, and no one's reported a male of that age going off on a jaunt, except for a callout last night that's interesting."

"How so?"

"Glen and Tory went to a butcher's shop in town. The lad who works there had forgotten his phone and went back to get it. An Owen Givens. Long story short, the shop was unsecured and the butcher nowhere to be seen. Uniform have been round there again this morning — still no sign of anyone. Owen popped in earlier to give a proper statement. His major concern was a water hose being put away wrong, which to him indicates there's something up with the butcher, Dave Johnson. Owen seems to think Dave wouldn't have left it like that."

"So basically, it's iffy."

"Well, yeah, considering the back door was also unlocked, as was the rear yard gate. Oh, and something about the curtains in the flat upstairs. Dave always shuts them once it starts getting dark. They weren't closed. As far as Tory and Glen are concerned, it's dodgy because it seems this Dave didn't have any dinner, so the guess is, someone came into the shop and . . . did whatever. The takings were in the till, so not a robbery. Johnson apparently clears the till out after each shift, so for that money to still be there, we're talking between five and half past when someone entered the shop and, well, maybe took the butcher. Owen left at five, see."

"Is Dave Johnson on our database?"

"No, clean as a whistle."

"Okay. We'll deal with the grave issue first, then nip to the butcher's. Can't hurt for us to have a look around."

"Forensics have decided to go there — another reason why I'm ringing you, so you might not feel the need to go. There are spots of blood. Now, obviously it could be from an animal, given the nature of the business, but with the lad convinced this whole scenario is unlike Dave, Isabelle decided to send one of her teams in and asked me to let you know. She's at the other site, the cemetery."

"Lovely. Two cases at once. If you can go back to the grave info . . ."

"Yep. There are signs of it being dug up. Lots of mud, wet as eff, along the side where it was dumped then put back in. With the weather last night and today, the ground sodden, we've been lucky. Footprints."

"Brilliant."

"Male, going by the size — ten at an estimate. No witnesses, though. Unlikely anyway. That storm came in pretty quickly, didn't it."

"It did. Which cemetery is it?"

"The one on Wallflower Road. Nothing opposite and either side but fields."

"Okay, I'll grab Mike, then we'll get down there. Tarra for now."

She put her phone away. Mike was already looking at her, resignation clear in his expression.

"We've got two things to deal with, people." Bethany explained what was going on at both scenes. "So, Leona and Fran, park the visit to Laura Tremmings for now — palm it off on uniforms if they have the time. Tammy, bin the CPS report until you have a minute. You all need to get on with searches for the following." She turned to the whiteboards and picked up a marker. "One, poke into a Dave Johnson, the butcher. Two, a worker, Owen Givens — let's see if he's on our radar. Tammy, I want you on the third thing: any recent grave disturbances going back, say, two years and spanning one hundred miles at first, then try farther afield." She scribbled it all on the board. "Me and Mike will visit the grave, seeing as there's a body there, albeit in parts, the poor sod."

The girls got to work, and Bethany put on her coat then led the way out of the incident room to the main doors downstairs. Rain lashed down, and she legged it across the car park. The wind had a mind to keep tugging her hood off, and her hair got wet. In the car, she buckled up along with Mike, then gave the engine a rev and switched the wipers on. She'd have to drive carefully, even though she wanted to get to the cemetery fast, the weather was unpredictable and likely to bring a few accidents to the emergency services' attention today.

She drove off, the sky an angry grey, bordering on black in places, and thunder boomed. "Bloody hell, we have a drumroll accompaniment for a spooky location. Thunder, a storm, and a cemetery. Couldn't get more hackneyed if we tried."

Mike laughed. "All we need is lightning and we'll be set."

"Stop it. It said on the telly lightning was due. So what do you make of this then? The body, I mean."

Mike wiped some rain off his forehead. Pearls of it sat in his hair. "It's an easy place to dispose of a body when you think about it. The ground's already been dug up recently, so less work. A bit of elbow grease removing mud, pop your bags in, then cover it up. Stupid, though, to have done it in the rain, leaving your footprints behind."

"Hmm, if it hadn't been for the mess, maybe the groundskeeper wouldn't have spotted anything. And those footprints might even be his. I bet he's bodged the scene right up. As for disposing of the body in this weather, perhaps they had nowhere to store it. Maybe they're knowledgeable about what happens with a grave — when the ground settles, when the turf gets put on. They could have been keeping tabs and knew grass would be laid soon, so they had to dump their kill as soon as possible."

"Got to be a savage bastard to chop someone up, don't you think?"

"And have the right tools to do it." She thought about the other case. "Fucking hell, the butcher's . . . Bit of a stretch, me hoping they're linked?"

"Nah, it makes sense. We'd be dim not to consider it."

"True."

They continued in silence, and after a few minutes, she turned into the cemetery and parked behind the SOCO van. An officer was at the back of it, ferreting about inside for something or other, so they asked him for protectives and got on with the business of suiting up. While she slid on gloves, the last thing she had to put on, she stared across at the tent, which battled valiantly to stay upright in the vicious wind despite the metal pegs holding it down. It billowed from sneaky gusts barging in through the front flaps, and Bethany caught a glimpse of Isabelle Abbott, the lead SOCO, on hands and knees.

They walked towards the log officer, Nicola Eccles, hunched inside a thick black poncho that at least kept the majority of her dry. She stood in front of a cordon that was strung up between two poplars, the tape flapping so madly it thrummed out an annoying buzz. Managing to sign in regardless of the rain plopping on the screen, Bethany then walked to the tent, glancing over her shoulder to check for the ME's red car, but no, Presley Zouche wasn't here yet.

She entered, glad to be out of the downpour, although it was still slightly blustery inside. "Morning."

Isabelle peered up from her perch, a step on the ground to preserve any evidence, most likely one of the footprints. "Afternoon, more like. It's after twelve."

"Ooh, are you Miss Pedantic today?" Bethany raised her eyebrows at the same time as putting the face mask in place.

"No, just saying. If it's afternoon, it means the end of the day is closer." Isabelle stood. "Not that the end of our day is going to be at the usual time."

"I know. What have we got here?"

Mike came in and stood beside Bethany. "A bloody mess by the looks of it."

Isabelle smiled. "That's because the groundsman, bless his heart, sarcasm and middle finger emoji fully present, spotted part of a black bag and decided to push the mud aside. He then opened the bag to see if someone had just been disrespectful and dumped rubbish here — and yes, that'd be weird in itself — and he discovered a leg, chopped at the knee joint, so two pieces in all. While I can understand why he did it, he really has fucked things up."

"Where is he?"

"Having a coffee and a calm down in his little hut. When you go out of here, turn right, follow the path, and you'll see it." Isabelle rubbed her forehead with the back of her gloved hand. "Some of the footprints are his, but those over there—"she pointed to the right — "belong to someone else. Different size and tread."

"What sex is the deceased?" Mike asked.

"Male. About sixty." Isabelle grinned. "His head's in that bag there if you want to see it."

"Bloody hell." Bethany *didn't* want to see it, but she'd be better off with a visual to match to an image of Dave Johnson when she got one. "Go on then."

Isabelle walked across a couple of evidence steps and opened one of the bags. Bethany gasped. The cheeks had hooks embedded in them, the sort dead animals hung from. This *had* to be related to the butcher's shop incident. If it wasn't, it was a damn creepy coincidence.

"Oh blimey," Mike muttered.

The victim's neck had been severed with a clean slice, and Bethany needed to get to the shop in order to see what kind of tools were used on the meat. Would there be a sharp enough, big enough knife that would cut through like this? If it *was* extra-sharp, did that mean the person didn't need to be particularly strong?

"Are all the other parts so cleanly cut?" she asked.

"Yes, so someone knows exactly what they're doing," Isabelle said. "Like another butcher — yep, I'm thinking this is related to the other scene."

Could Owen Givens have done this? She wished she'd asked Rob on her way out of the station for the lad's statement. His alibi would be in there, and she could either discount him or sit him firmly in the frame.

"Two seconds." She phoned Rob. "Hi. Where was Owen Givens last night before he went to the butcher's shop?"

"Hang on. Let me just get the file up . . . Ah, here we go. The Flapping Crow from six thirty until nine twenty. Glen and Tory went to the pub last night. CCTV's installed there because of fighting. Leona's asked for the high street footage, so she's probably checking where he went after he left the Crow."

"Cheers." She put her phone away. "Okay, let's say this fella here is the butcher. It's looking unlikely his assistant is involved. He left the pub at nine twenty, so unless he's super-fast in killing someone and chopping them up, he wouldn't have had time to bury him between then and making the nine-nine-nine call, especially if he had to clean up afterwards. Now, Rob said the takings are usually dealt with at half five, and the money was still in the till. Owen can't have done anything to Dave at five either — again, no time to kill, cut up, and clean before he entered the pub about half six."

"So someone else then," Mike said. "A disgruntled customer?"

"Fucking hell, a customer with that much knife knowledge?" Isabelle blurted. "Or what, did he give them a fatty steak or one sausage short of what they needed and they got arsey? Who the hell gets *that* upset with a butcher?"

"You know full well people get funny about the smallest things," Bethany said. "The last straw is usually ridiculous."

"But to have knowledge of how to cut someone up?" Isabelle shook her head. "Come on now."

"I agree, it's likely to be another butcher, but who? A rival?" Bethany got her phone out again and messaged Fran to look up butchers in the area. She pressed SEND then returned her attention to the others. "So Dave Johnson was taking business off them? This might not even *be* Johnson." She prodded the air towards the head. "We need a photo." She sent another message to Fran, asking if she could find any images of him. "What else is off here?"

"Well, as you can see, that face is clean, so if we're going with the idea this is Johnson, he was washed at the shop before transportation, or wherever. There are specks of blood at the butcher's. If they match the DNA from here . . . The rest of the body parts I've seen are clean as well, so someone had a good go at washing it."

Bethany bobbed her head. "Hmm, you may be right. Rob mentioned a hose being put back wrong."

"I'm willing to bet it was used to wash the chopping area," Isabelle said. "Now, before I forget to tell you, I've had some images sent to me by my team there." She handed her phone over. "I'd say have a butcher's at them, but even I know that pun is below the belt."

"Sodding Nora, Izz. Did you have to go that low?" Despite trying not to, Bethany smiled and accessed Isabelle's picture gallery — luckily the screen worked fine with her gloved finger.

"Can't help myself." Isabelle chuckled.

"If any civvies ever heard us, we'd sound a right bunch of unfeeling bastards," Mike said.

"They'd act the same after a while in this job." Bethany stared down at the phone.

The first image was of the hose. It was a jumble — put away in a rush? And wasn't the killer brazen if they'd killed while both exits had been unlocked? Was that part of the thrill, getting caught? Or did they just not care? Maybe they'd locked up while killing then opened the exits again.

The second picture was of the blood specks, the third a white-tiled wall with various knives and cleavers held up by a thick magnetic strip. One of the larger cleavers was wonky, the rest in a regimented row. Interesting. Was the one used to chop the body put back in haste, hence it being skew-whiff? A saw — *Jesus Christ!* — hung from a hook. She supposed that hadn't been used due to the noise it would make, but with the wind howling down the high street, would it have been heard? She'd bet not many people had been out and about.

Other images revealed nothing much.

"That cleaver there," she said, showing Isabelle the image.

"Already been taken in as evidence." Isabelle took her phone. "It looked odd, not being straight in the line. All the tools have gone to the lab. Sorry, but when I got here and saw the clean cuts, I put two and two together. This has *got* to be related to the butcher's shop, and if it isn't, let you two be my witnesses when I say I'll eat a gherkin if it isn't."

"You hate gherkins," Mike said.

"That's how sure I am." Isabelle winked.

"I agree with you, Izz, so no gherkins necessary." Bethany nodded. "And now we have to find out who the hell did this."

"We're just about to dig deeper." Isabelle indicated the grave by flapping her hand. "We obviously need to check the coffin hasn't been tampered with — and won't that be a bugger if it has?"

Bethany's guts rolled. She hadn't expected this to happen. Biting her lip, she stood back while the body parts, still in their bags, were placed in plastic evidence sacks then put inside what looked like huge Tupperware boxes and labelled. All the while, she chatted to Mike, throwing out possibilities to take her mind off the officers digging up the mud.

She jumped at the bleep of her phone and accessed the message, thankful for something to do.

Fran: IMAGE INCOMING OF DAVE JOHNSON, SENT FROM SOCO AT THE BUTCHER'S — HE HAD ONE OF HIMSELF BEHIND THE COUNTER ON THE WALL NEXT TO SOME CERTIFICATES IN FRAMES. OWEN GIVENS' CAR IS SEEN AT A RED LIGHT EARLIER IN THE EVENING, LIKE HE SAID, PLUS HE'S ON CCTV WALKING DOWN THE HIGH STREET LATER AND FALLING INTO THE SHOP — I'M GUESSING THE WIND SHOVED HIM. GLEN AND TORY ARRIVE NOT LONG AFTER. NO DISTURBED GRAVES REPORTED WITHIN ONE HUNDRED MILES, SO TAMMY'S WIDENED THE SEARCH. THERE ARE TWO OTHER BUTCHER SHOPS IN TOWN — LEN STOBBART'S AT THE OTHER END OF THE HIGH STREET AND THOMAS VALTON IN THE SHOPPING CENTRE.

Bethany: THANKS.

Another bleep heralded the receipt of the picture. She opened it. Yes, this was him all right. He looked so kindly it hurt her heart that someone had done this to him. "Positive ID on the victim. It's Dave Johnson."

Isabelle glanced up from her position next to the grave. "We've got a bigger problem."

Bethany stared at the deep hole where the mud had been removed. The coffin lid was placed on a clean sheet of plastic. She didn't want to look into the coffin itself but knew she'd have to. She did, and the damn thing was empty. "Fucking hell . . ." She took in the name on the grave marker that stood in place of a stone for now. "Angela Lockwood, where the hell are you?"

CHAPTER FOUR

Owen was at a loss as to what to do now he had no work today. That copper, Glen Underby, had phoned him first thing to let him know the shop was definitely classed as a crime scene and that he should stay away until further notice. He'd received no news about Dave, which concerned him a hell of a lot. What, had someone gone in there and kidnapped him? Why? Dave didn't have any enemies as far as Owen knew, he was too nice for that, and as for the takings being left behind, it didn't make sense. There had to have been a fair old whack in that till, what with everyone coming in to stock up, so why not take advantage and steal it?

He'd messaged Charlotte, telling her what had happened, and she'd asked if he needed to have a chat. He was relieved she'd suggested it, which saved him having to ask and coming off as needy. It might scare her off him if he was a wet lettuce. They'd agreed to meet in the Flapping Crow for lunch, although he'd need to be careful how much he spent, seeing as he wasn't earning for the foreseeable. His mum would see him right if he needed a tenner here and there, but that was beside the point when she didn't earn a packet herself. He still lived at home so was a burden enough as it was.

He got in his car and drove to the high street, lucky enough to grab a parking spot in front of the pub. Owen dashed across the pavement, the rain sneaking inside his collar, and once inside, he wiped his neck. He found Charlotte sitting where they had last night, a phone and the last knockings of a Coke in front of her. She swiped her thumb across the screen a few times and raised her head as if sensing his arrival.

"Are you okay?" She gave him a sympathetic look.

He sat and sighed, rubbing the bridge of his nose. He had a nasty headache, his eyes sore from lack of sleep, his jaw tight where he kept clenching it. "I'll be all right once they find Dave."

She reached out to pat his hand. "Was it scary going in and giving a statement?"

"Yep, but it had to be done, no getting away from it, is there. I'm not taking the blame for this. I did nothing wrong, but it feels like they think I did. Or maybe I'm just being paranoid."

"I would be, too, but they probably have to suspect everyone. You might have been the last to see him, don't forget."

"I suppose." So he didn't dwell on that and get himself even more stewed up, he said, "Want another Coke?" He glanced at her near-empty glass.

"Please. It's your turn to pay, so I'll have a cheese and onion baguette and a bowl of chips and cheese."

"You and your cheese." He smiled and went to the bar to order, getting himself a Coke as well, even though he could do with having a triple Bacardi in it, but the last thing he needed was to be pulled over for driving while under the influence on top of all the other shit going on. That'd look awful, and maybe like he was guilty if he got pissed up. God, he'd be double-checking all his actions from now on just in case they made him seem bad.

He returned to the table, tired of all the shit going round in his head, and they chatted about where Dave could have gone, or whether someone had taken him, and if so, who? It was good to speak to someone about it. Mum was at work, so he hadn't even had her to talk to. Mind you, the copper he'd given his statement to this morning had been nice.

Their food arrived, and another fifteen minutes dribbled by while they ate.

"I hope he's okay, I really do," Charlotte said.

"Me, too." Was it selfish of him to hope it was all a misunderstanding and Dave would come back, happy as Larry after taking some time out? Owen needed to work, needed the wages. His mum couldn't carry them both for long, not on her pay. Things could go downhill fast once his pennies stopped coming in. They'd be eating a lot of beans on toast, *and* he wouldn't get the offcuts of meat Dave always gave him for free.

Her phone screen lit up on the table, MUM on a blue bar in the centre, and her ringtone blared out.

"Bugger. Won't be a sec." She answered the call, her cheeks going pale. "W-what?" A pause, eyes wide, going wider still. "Oh my God! Yes . . . Okay . . . I'm coming now. Please don't worry, all right?" She swiped her screen and stared at Owen, lips parted.

"What's the matter?" His heart thudded a bit painfully.

Charlotte's bottom lip wobbled, and tears shone, ready to fall. "That was my mum. The police are there."

"What for?"

She blinked. "It's our old neighbour. She's been taken out of her grave. Can you bloody believe that?"

Owen's heart lurched and pounded even harder. What the hell was going on around here? First Dave, and now this. "Fucking hell. Who'd want to do that?"

"That's not all of it." She shoved her phone in her bag on the floor, draped the handle over her shoulder, and stood. "Body parts in black bags were put there instead."

"Fucking hell . . ."

"And they're Dave's, *your* Dave's."

If Owen was standing, he'd have sat pretty sharpish. His legs went weak, his skin cold, and his chest tightened. "Dave? Dave the butcher?"

Charlotte nodded. "I have to go . . ."

"Shall I come with you?"

"No, I'll text you later."

Charlotte ran off, leaving Owen in complete shock.

Someone had killed Dave and dumped him. He couldn't bloody believe this!

CHAPTER FIVE

Bethany smiled at Valerie Howard, who'd just come off the phone. Once Bethany had cottoned on that she was the mother of Charlotte, the woman Owen Givens had met last night in the pub, she'd asked her to call her daughter. Bethany could chat to Charlotte about Owen at the same time as asking her if she knew of anyone who would have wanted to dig up her mum's next-door neighbour.

Angela Lockwood had died after a short illness, unmarried, no family, no children, having devoted her life to other people's — a teacher in one of the secondary schools. Bethany got chills at the thought of someone perhaps watching the funeral, planning to remove her from the coffin and put Dave Johnson in the hole instead. You had to be a special kind of deranged to do what had been done.

"I can't believe this is happening." Valerie's voice wavered, and she gave her nose a wipe with a scrunched tissue, one she'd been using to dab at her eyes since Bethany had dropped the bombshell. "It's like a nightmare."

"I understand."

Bethany thought of her husband, Vinny, and how surreal it had all felt when he'd died in a house fire he'd been called out to. She empathised with Valerie and wished she hadn't had to come here, but with Angela having no next of kin, Leona had suggested trying the neighbours in the street where Angela had lived. They'd questioned everyone and come up trumps with Valerie, who was a good friend of Angela's.

Bethany decided to move things along. "So before you rang Charlotte, you were saying you knew Dave Johnson."

"Yes, he was in Angela's form at school — they're a few years older than me. Obviously, none of us moved away since we grew up. Then, of course, he's the butcher. I prefer his stuff more than Stobbart's so go to Dave instead. Charlotte generally nips in there to get a steak for the dog, too." She glanced at the little long-haired mixed breed curled up on the rug, its fur a blend of cream, brown, and black. "That's where she met Owen."

"How long has she been seeing him?"

"Oh, I think that was their third date last night, maybe the fourth, I'm not sure. Charlotte really likes him. She says he isn't the same as the other lads. He isn't into getting drunk and whatever." She covered her mouth. "Oh. Do you think he had anything to do with Dave's murder?"

Mike cleared his throat. "We doubt it very much."

"Thank God." She lowered her hand to her lap. "Charlotte would be so upset if she had to stop seeing him. He doesn't sound the type anyway, to be honest."

What was 'the type', though? The majority of killers Bethany had dealt with, and it was a fair few now, had seemed pleasant when spoken to. They'd hidden their true natures — not surprising, otherwise they'd have been suspects earlier — and had appeared nice enough, although a couple had given her vibes, and she'd looked at them closely after that. But there weren't facial characteristics they all had that identified them as killers. Not everyone inclined to murder had mad staring eyes that were too close together or a hard mouth that rarely smiled.

"I'm sure he isn't the sort to do anything like this," Bethany said.

A key sliding into a lock filtered through from the hallway, and a young woman appeared, walking into the living room. She'd been crying, that much was clear, and she rushed over to sit on the sofa beside Valerie, the dog prancing about, happy she was home.

"Are you okay, Mum?"

"In shock, but it's okay. I'm okay." Valerie patted Charlotte's hand. "It's Angela I'm thinking about. No one knows where she's gone or who took her."

"This is so horrible." Charlotte shivered. "Poor Owen was gobsmacked when I told him Dave was in the cemetery."

Bethany winced. Great. If Owen *was* involved, he now knew Dave had been discovered. Then again, the killer could be watching. Some got a kick out of doing that.

But you don't think it's him anyway, so what's the problem?

The problem was that Owen's name was also attached to *this* side of the investigation. He was seeing the daughter of Angela's dug-up neighbour, for God's sake. A macabre coincidence, perhaps just plain old back luck for him, but all the same . . .

"You were with Owen last night, I understand," Bethany said to Charlotte.

She nodded. "Yes. We had dinner at the Flapping Crow." She gave the times and confirmed that Owen had been late, had lost his phone, and had walked down the high street to the butcher's after he'd seen her to her car.

A gentleman then, making sure she got to her vehicle safely. He went up in Bethany's estimation.

"Thanks. So did you message him about Dave before coming here?"

"No, I was in the pub with him again, having lunch. We'd met up because he was struggling with what might have happened to Dave. We've been texting this morning — I think he just needed someone to chat to. Would you like to see?" She fished her phone out of her bag.

"That'd be great, yes."

Charlotte accessed her texts and handed the phone over.

Owen: SORRY TO SOUND SUCH A WIMP, BUT I NEED SOMEONE TO TALK TO. WHEN I WENT BACK TO THE SHOP LAST NIGHT TO GET MY PHONE, THE DOORS WERE UNLOCKED AND DAVE WASN'T THERE. I HAD TO PHONE THE POLICE BECAUSE IT WAS WELL OFF.

> Charlotte: OMG, I HOPE HE'S ALL RIGHT. WHAT DID THE POLICE SAY?

Owen: THEY'RE LOOKING INTO IT, AND I'VE JUST BEEN DOWN THE STATION TO GIVE A STATEMENT. I'M WORRIED THEY THINK I DID SOMETHING TO HIM, BUT I WAS WITH YOU, AND WHY WOULD I DO ANYTHING? HE'S A NICE BLOKE.

> Charlotte: TELL THEM MY NAME. I'LL BACK YOU UP.

Owen: I ALREADY DID.

> Charlotte: GOOD. AND THERE'S THAT BARMAID AS WELL. SHE'LL REMEMBER US BECAUSE YOU SPILT YOUR BEER AND SHE HAD TO COME AND CLEAN THE TABLE.

Owen: I FORGOT ABOUT THAT.

> Charlotte: DO YOU WANT TO MEET FOR LUNCH?

Owen: YEAH. I CAN'T GO TO WORK AS IT'S A CRIME SCENE. THEY MUST HAVE FOUND SOMETHING. FUCK ME, I'M SO WORRIED ABOUT HIM.

Charlotte: I BET. OKAY, THE CROW. I CAN GET THERE ABOUT TEN PAST ONE.

Owen: THANKS. SEE YOU THEN.

Bethany gave the phone back. "How was he when you met him today?"

"He's paranoid you lot think he did something. I told him it's just unfortunate he went back there and the place was unlocked."

"He obviously found his phone, otherwise he wouldn't have been able to text you."

"Yes, it was on the shelf where he'd left it. Dave's was by the weighing machine."

So as well as money in the till, the killer had ignored two mobiles. This gave it a personal slant, indicating a different reason for killing Dave, and to be honest, even if they'd gone there to rob him and ended up, for whatever reason, not taking the money, cutting him up and putting him in a grave was extreme. A thief would have just knocked him out, killed him if that was their jam, stolen what they wanted, and left him there.

"Okay. I asked your mum this, but is there anyone you know of who may have wanted to remove Angela from the cemetery?"

"No. I can't imagine who'd want to do that to her." Charlotte bit her lip. "So if they took Angela, it seems obvious to me that the same person put Dave there. It's stupid to say two separate people happened to go to that grave — that they both even had the idea of *using* the grave."

Charlotte's reasoning put Bethany's mind at rest. She'd been thinking along similar lines, so having someone confirm the ridiculousness of imagining two people had the exact same idea was a comfort.

"I agree," she said. "Where is Owen now?"

"I left him in the pub."

Bethany focused on Valerie. "Based on you saying you were close to Angela, had she given you any idea that someone held a grudge against her?"

"No. She was so nice. She had nothing derogatory to say about our other neighbours or her colleagues. She was the sort who looked for the best in everyone, and if she found a mean side to them, she'd offer reasons as to why they might be behaving that way. Honestly, she was a saint. In all the years I've known her, she's never bad-mouthed anyone."

So perhaps her grave had been targeted simply because it was new, nothing to do with who occupied the coffin at all. The thing Bethany couldn't get to grips with was, if they'd just needed somewhere to put Dave, why remove Angela when they hadn't even placed Dave inside the coffin? Why take her out, put the lid back on, refill the hole, dump the bags, then cover them with mud? It was all a bit like hard work in her mind. The easier route was Dave could have been left exactly where he had been, leaving Angela to rest in peace.

A puzzle to solve.

The dog skipped over to Mike, who crouched to fuss the animal. "Silly bugger, aren't you, eh?"

"He was Angela's." Valerie sighed as if all the fight had gone out of her. "There was no one else down the street willing to take him, and a shelter wasn't something I'd entertain. We've known him five years since she brought him home as a pup, so it was the best thing for him, coming here. He's attached to Charlotte."

"He's attached to the steak I buy him, not me." Charlotte smiled.

Valerie nodded absently. "Charlotte's been buying it ever since Angela got ill, so Angela didn't worry the dog was missing out. It was something Angela always did, getting the steak."

That was interesting. "Did Angela get it from Dave Johnson?"

"She did."

So if Angela was a regular customer, what if someone had heard her talking to Dave about being ill, dying? The eavesdropper could have had the idea of using her grave. It was supposition, but that was better than having no leads whatsoever. Unfortunately, with the number of customers Dave must have had, narrowing down one with sinister intentions would be nigh on impossible — unless Owen could help them.

Bethany rose. "Well, we must get off now. Again, sorry for your loss and for us even being here today."

"That's not your fault," Valerie said.

"I'll see you out." Charlotte got up and led the way to the front door, the mutt hot on her heels. She turned to them with her hand on the knob. "I can almost guarantee it isn't Owen. I'm not some stupid girl who's fallen for him and won't hear a nasty word said. I'm a realist, and he hasn't got a bad bone in his body."

"Thanks. We'll bear that in mind." Bethany left and waited for Mike to join her in the car. "Seeing as we've spoken to the other neighbours already, what d'you reckon about going to see Owen?"

"You think it's him?"

"Nope, but I want to pick his brains about customers." She told him her theory while messaging Fran for Owen's address. "Too far-fetched?"

"Not at all. If someone had the intention to kill Dave but didn't know where they could put the body, knowing Angela was recently buried could have been all they needed for the idea to be put in their mind. Why *remove* Angela, though?"

"I'm struggling with that." She accessed her message app and prodded the address into the satnav. Then she pulled away, straining to see — the rain had decided to pelt down so hard it bounced back up off the road. It drummed on the car roof as if knocking to come in.

"Doesn't make sense to me at all," Mike said. "You get rid of one body but take another — so that means your theory is a bit off. They *must* have somewhere to take bodies if they have Angela."

"Okay, bear with me here, because what I've just thought is gross, but it's a possibility. Necrophilia."

"What, someone took Angela to have *sex* with her?" Mike shuddered. "Fucking hell. And would you look at that rain. Pull over for a bit until it eases off."

She did that, parking in a residential street. "Or what about this. They fancied Angela, maybe had a crush on her for however long, and having her with them dead is better than not at all."

"Disgusting, but I see where you're coming from. We've dealt with some right weird people, so someone doing this wouldn't surprise me. I'll feel sick if that turns out to be the case, though."

"It's vile, but we need to come up with ideas, otherwise we'll get stuck and won't move forward." She stared at the windscreen, water covering it in a rippled sheet now the violence of it had eased. "It could just be a coincidence, too, the chosen grave, so let's think about that for a minute. With no other grave disturbances reported, we'll say this is the first time for the killer. They watch the cemetery a lot to see who's been buried. We should go back there and talk to the groundsman, really, before we see Owen. With CCTV on Owen's side, he's basically in the clear. All we'd be doing is verifying his statement and asking about customers. Actually, I'll get Tammy to give him a bell."

"Good idea."

She sent her a message then drove off. They arrived at the cemetery, and she parked where she had before. Presley's car was there, so they suited up and headed for the tent first. Inside, Presley was just taking the temperature of an arm in one of the plastic boxes, and it looked so wrong in there, Bethany had the urge to cry.

"Afternoon," she said to him, giving Isabelle a pointed look as if to say: *I got the time of day right, madam.*

Isabelle stuck her tongue out.

"Hello, you two." Presley studied the temp instrument. "Okay, I'm going to say this man died between five and six thirty yesterday evening."

Bethany thought about that for a moment. "Right, so that tells us Dave didn't lock up or do the takings because he was being offed. Would you say it'd take a while to chop the body up?"

"Butcher's tools are seriously sharp." Presley rose and picked up his notebook to scribble something down. "The way this body was cut, it feels systematic, as though there was no dilly-dallying — they knew what they were doing."

"Dilly-dallying!" Isabelle laughed. "Did you swallow an old-fashioned dictionary, Pres?"

Presley didn't bite. He was getting good at ignoring Isabelle when she tried to wind him up, which was often and at nearly every scene. "They knew where to cut, which tells me they've perhaps studied joints, muscles, tendons et cetera. Each slice is at the easiest point to hack through."

"Like I said, another butcher." Isabelle paraded a smug grin, her mouth mask down by her neck.

"We'll have to speak to this Len Stobbart fella, and Thomas Volton, see if there was a meat war," Mike said.

"A meat war?" Isabelle roared with laughter, bending double. "Oh my bloody good God."

"You can joke," Bethany said. "But people kill over the silliest things. Anyway, much as it's nice to natter, we need to go and speak to the groundsman."

"Sausages at dawn, not pistols," Isabelle chortled out.

Bethany shook her head, left the tent, and walked with a chuckling Mike along the path that curved around a jam-packed area of the cemetery — so many gravestones, so many people missed by loved ones. At the end, near some iron gates, stood a stone building, one-story, which had perhaps been a small home back in the day. She knocked on the wooden door shiny from rain, and it opened on creaking hinges, another addition to the already creepy surroundings and weather that leant an ominous air to everything.

The gentleman who stood there must be closing in on seventy, his hair wispy and white, his cheeks ruddy. His khaki-coloured fisherman's rib jumper looked as if it kept him warm, and his combats had camouflage print on them, but faded, as if he'd washed them a hundred times. Clean wellies encased his feet — Isabelle had probably taken the boots he'd had on at the graveside.

She got out her ID and held it up for him. "I'm DI Bethany Smith, and this is my partner, DS Mike Wilkins. And you are?"

"Harold Morgan."

"Can we come inside?"

"Yep. Get yourselves in out of this weather."

The short hallway had a room either side. She glimpsed tools and whatnot in the one on the left, and a staffroom, for want of a better word, on the right. He took them in there and sat on a red tartan chair beside the fire, which crackled and belted out a decent amount of heat and the faint whiff of smoke. Glad of a chance to park her backside, she chose the other chair while Mike stood by the window.

"I know you've given a statement to our colleagues, but we're here to ask something else." Bethany smiled. "Have you seen anyone hanging around here lately? Specifically when there's a funeral on?"

"Can't say I have, no. Funerals are busy times. Lots of people. They walk along the paths, chatter in groups. For some of them, it's the first time they've seen a family member in years, so they reminisce and whatnot. All strangers to me, apart from those who've spoken to me beforehand about buying a plot."

"So no person has come back often, who perhaps looks out of place? Let's say they don't have a grave they visit, they just walk around."

"That would be a bit strange and something I'd notice. I'm normally out there, making sure everything's neat and tidy. That's how I spotted that grave had been tampered with. I had to check none of the trees had come down in the wind. Yesterday, the mud was flat, just like it was the day she was buried. I expected subsidence because of the rain weighting it, dragging it down, but no. Today it was lumpy, and I knew something was under there. Then I saw the black bag sticking out. It wouldn't be the first time someone's dumped their rubbish in a grave — sick, I know, but there you have it, people do the strangest things so long as they get the desired end result. Doesn't matter if it's someone's loved one under the ground when they bury their bean tins and whatnot in there. So I ripped one open and . . ." He shuddered, going pale.

She supposed he'd seen the bag contents in his head. "Has anything else seemed off lately?"

"Now I come to think of it, yes. The padlocks were changed on the gate behind this place. Twice. Yesterday morning I thought I was going a bit senile and had forgotten that I'd put a new padlock on there — it was shinier, and the key was dangling from it. But when it happened this morning an' all . . . Someone had to have broken in and put new locks on."

"Yes, otherwise, they'd have had to drop the bags over then climb in."

"I'd say the bags would have split if they were dropped, wouldn't you, all that weight in them?"

"Definitely."

"Would you like a drink? I've got a kettle there, see, and I can make you a brew."

Bethany glanced up at Mike. He nodded. She was glad he felt the same as her. This old man needed company after the shock he'd had, and they could spare the time it took to sip a coffee.

"That would be lovely, Harold," she said. "Really lovely."

CHAPTER SIX

"Your mother's a whore."

Roland stared at the man who towered over him. Lee Didsbrough. Mr Nice Guy — to the outsider.

"She didn't care about you. Otherwise, why leave, eh? Why bloody well leave?"

As young as he was, Roland knew why she'd left. She'd found a new man, so Daddy said time and time again, like he didn't want Roland to forget it. A new someone she loved more than her own son. More than her husband. She was a bitch and a cow, according to him, a selfish one at that, but Roland didn't believe that was true, not to begin with. How could she be selfish when she'd read to him before bed, giving up her time for him, and had handed him her share of cakes or sweets when money was scarce? Daddy's business had gone through a bad patch once, what with the foot-and-mouth outbreak, whatever that was.

The day she'd left, she'd walked him to school with a purple bruise on her temple, holding his hand, same as she always did. Roland had felt safe by the main road, despite the whooshing cars and lorries, the odd motorbike haring past at breakneck speed. Mummy wouldn't let him get hurt by them — she took position on the outside of the path so he was farthest from the danger. She'd said she'd get hit first if a vehicle mounted the kerb, and he'd be saved.

At school, she'd settled him in his classroom, then hugged him tight, a big cuddle that squeezed the air out of him, and, breathless, he'd clung on, wishing it was just her and him at home. No Daddy shouting. No Daddy throwing his fists about. No Daddy touching Roland's maggot. He couldn't remember a time when he hadn't touched it, and he'd been tempted to ask Mummy why it happened but remembered Daddy saying he mustn't tell her. So instead he'd asked his friends if they liked their dad playing with them.

"Yeah, my dad plays football with me in the garden," one had said. "He's the goalie, and I have to score."

"Mine asks me to do jigsaw puzzles, and sometimes we play noughts and crosses."

That had been confusing. No one else's father played with maggots, only games. Was that why it had to be a secret? Why he'd been told never to speak about it to anyone but Daddy?

"I'm going to fix everything," she'd said after the cuddle. "Make it so nothing bad happens again."

Roland had blinked up at her, not understanding what she'd meant.

"It's just you and me," Daddy said now. "And don't you forget who stayed, who takes care of you. Be grateful one of us stuck around."

At the sound of that voice, Roland blinked away the memories. The two years since she'd gone had dragged past, every day difficult to get through. Every day left with him, *the daddy unlike any other. Roland cried every night.*

He supposed he should be grateful, like Daddy had said. Some kids got put into the foster system with strangers. There was a girl in his class who stayed with people who weren't her mum and dad. She could only go back to her real home if her parents showed they could behave themselves. They must have been naughty or something. She used to come to school with circle burns on the backs of her hands, scabby, they were, but they'd healed up now, and she smiled ever such a lot lately.

Foster care wasn't for him, though, the uncertainty of the unknown. At least he knew what was coming at home. He knew his father's moods, his patterns, his strange behaviour, his need to teach Roland to be 'manly'. New people would be weird, and he wouldn't understand them for ages, not until he'd watched them for a while.

Daddy swigged straight from a vodka bottle. "Two years today, Rebecca." He stared at the ceiling as though she was up there and could hear him. He always did that, looked up, even outside, like she was in the sky or something, watching from behind the stars.

Roland didn't nod, didn't dare speak.

"You're gone, woman," Daddy slurred. "You left me." He flung himself on the sofa, the liquid sloshing inside the bottle.

The story was always the same, it never deviated. At first, the lady neighbours had asked where Mummy was. They hadn't seen her around recently, and with Daddy taking Roland to school in the car now, they knew something was up. Daddy had acted the nice man, something he always did with everyone else. He was kind to the people who came in his shop, too. Only Roland saw his other side.

"Rebecca's walked out on us." Pitiful expression. Eyes watering. "She's found someone else. I can't believe it. She seemed so happy here, so it just goes to show how she hid her real feelings. And to leave our Roland . . ." A shake of the head. "It beggars belief."

"Oh, Lee . . ." A hand pat. A downturned mouth. "I'm so very sorry . . . I thought everything was fine. She never said a word. I didn't realise . . ."

The women of the street were sorry enough to make casseroles and the occasional cake to begin with, and once, one of them had given Roland a big bag of sweets, but after a while those gifts stopped, as did the visits to make sure Daddy and Roland were okay. Life went on around their two-up, two-down in Jamaica Street, leaving Roland to suffer with the monster inside it— and those that loitered in his head, voices, angry voices that unsettled him sometimes with the things they said to him.

She didn't leave you.

She's out there.

He did this, not her.

She loved you.

"Show me your maggot," Daddy said.

Roland jumped. Pulled his trousers and pants down.

Daddy knocked back another mouthful of vodka. "Now come here beside me so I can lick your face."

* * *

Standing on his stepladder, Roland licked Angela's cheek, tears staining his, the memories bringing them on. She tasted riper today, the flavour spreading all over his tongue, into his saliva, into him. Her sticker smile told him she liked being licked, that she loved him and would never leave, but she would eventually, in a sense. While all the mummies were still here, they weren't the same as when he'd first hung them by their scalps on the hooks. Slowly, some of them had changed from looking like a person to something 'other', drying out, disintegrating, and although he knew Jen and Angela would go the same way and he'd miss them with flesh, the anticipation of meeting a new mummy always made up for it.

Nothing beat that first moment, the coffin lid removed, Mummy inside. The emotions that coursed through him then were as he'd imagined they would've been if Mummy had come back, tired of that man, realising Jamaica Street was where she really belonged.

He thought about *that* specific time, the Enlightenment, how it had explained so much, how horrific yet exhilarating it was. One half of him had been appalled, frightened, the other so happy he'd barely contained his excitement. He recreated that every time he dug up a body. It was his drug, his need, his salvation. So long as he could see Mummy for the first time in years again, everything would be okay.

"There, there," he said to Angela, who swung slightly from his lick. "It's all okay now. You're home. I'm here. We're together again."

Beside Angela, Jen remained still. Her sticker smile fell off, and he got down to pick it up off the floor. Was she jealous? Had her smile dropped because she was unhappy his attention was on Angela now? Well, if Jen wasn't rotting so quickly, reeking like that smell from rapid decomposition already, he wouldn't have had to collect Angela so soon, would he. Jen would have remained his number one for a while longer.

They'd all leave him in the end, becoming just bones, but as the flesh had sloughed off the earlier mums, he'd taken a piece and preserved it in vinegar, each jar in a line above the sink of his kitchenette, on a shelf he'd fashioned with a metal 'fence' around it so the jars didn't fall off when he drove. He had so many mummies and planned to dig one up for every year the real one had been gone.

He was owed almost a lifetime of mothers.

He went to his car and drew a new mouth for Jen. The other sticker was disgusting on the back, wet with a brown substance where her skin was going mushy and seeping some kind of rancid liquid. He had a grate on the floor of the artic, set lower down from the rest of the floor, adequate drainage, where fluids dripped out onto any number of verges he parked at, sinking onto the grass out of sight.

There was always a period where the stench bordered on being too much, and he had to leave the back door of the artic ajar overnight to release it. Not a good idea to do so during the day, when nosy people drove past, the scent filtering into their cars via the heater or through the open windows. Mind you, he always found out-of-the-way spots to park and hadn't had a problem so far.

It was all in the planning.

He got out of the Fiat and collected a couple of steak knives from the drawer beneath the little sink. He'd done this before on several occasions, and it would only work for so long. In front of Jen, he placed the sticker smile on her face then stabbed the knives in to hold it in place. Soon, her soft flesh of her cheeks would be all gone, scoffed by the maggots that came once flies got in, the knives falling out, and then the really bad smell would begin.

He inhaled a breath through his nose, letting the scent of death stick to the hairs in his nostrils. He liked it up there, reminding him, when he wasn't in the artic, what was waiting for him upon his return.

Glad Jen was smiling again, Roland took a steak out of the fridge and removed it from the bag. He rubbed it all over his face, enjoying the coldness, the blood that seeped out of it. A good lick of the red flesh had his maggot twitching, and he humped the air until down below got wet.

He sucked the blood out of the meat, swallowing it, then threw the steak in the bin. Beautiful. He used the toilet beside the kitchenette, one he'd taken out of a scrapped caravan at the breaker's yard in Southend, a tenner, a bargain price. It reminded him he'd need to empty the loo's holding tank soon, plus top up the water tank he'd installed. It was also attached to a caravan shower — thirty quid for that — which was next to the toilet, and his bed stood at the far end, down by the rear doors. A home in a row he liked to call it, and the mummies hung opposite, watching over him wherever he was in his little abode. He parked his Fiat just inside the doors, next to his bed, using a ramp when reversing it in or out. All in all, he had the perfect space, and he could drive away at a moment's notice, looking for all the world like any other trucker.

The money he'd received upon the sale of Daddy's butcher shop and his childhood home had been placed in his account, and he lived off the grid apart from his bank withdrawals, always from the ATM in the small shop at the end of Jamaica Street, Abingdon. He stayed in that area for three months of the year, enough time to withdraw the cash needed to live for the other nine months. He stopped digging up mummies at this point, always around the week when the Enlightenment had occurred.

It did him good to have a break.

His life was spent moving from town to town to city to village, getting to know the local butchers, watching the shops, learning their patterns, deciding which Daddy to kill. He spent time scouring the obituaries, attending the funerals of women, always standing at the back, an observer.

Handy info, those obits.

But lately something had changed. An urge to go on a spree, to do more than he usually did. It was getting harder to push those feelings aside. They'd begun to control him, and he might well give in to the calling.

Damn.

* * *

He studied the crowd, a big turnout for Susan Gorman, forty-three, a car accident taking her life, God rest her precious soul. The priest or whoever the hell presided over funerals droned on beside the grave, his voice an irritating grate on Roland's raw nerves.

Official men stood either side of the deep rectangular hole, holding thick straps that went under the coffin, and they slackened it as ashes to ashes, dust to dust was spewed out by the man of the cloth. Down Susan went in her wooden tomb with the shiny silver plaque, and Roland shivered with delight at coming here later to dig her up, take her back to his artic, and give her a good lick.

Then she was in the ground, and people stepped forward to throw mud, which clacked on the lid, loud and somehow rude on this quiet summer's day in a village outside Manchester, breaking up the sobs and wails slipping from wobbling mouths.

He stared, mesmerised, until someone came up to him, a woman of about forty, all brassy-blonde hair and drawn-on eyebrows, one higher than the other, as though she'd been pissed as a fart when she'd put them there using brown kohl.

"Hi, lovely of you to come. I'm Susan's sister."

He cursed himself for not spotting her approach sooner, but it was too late now. Of course, he could walk away, not say a word, but that would come off as odd, and if Susan being removed was ever discovered, this woman here might remember the man who'd remained silent and disappeared in his little Fiat.

She rubbed her arms as if cold, even though the sun was a raging bastard today. "How did you know Susan?"

Susan, the lady who rested inside that coffin, lucky enough to have a swarm of mourners all grieving, all caring. Susan, loved by all.

He wondered if she'd realised how lucky she was when she'd been alive. Had she been grateful for the love?

"Oh, we met at the library," he said. The obituary had mentioned her enjoyment of reading and how she'd helped out with the kids' club there. "She was good to my little girl." That had popped out of nowhere, but it seemed to do the trick.

The woman smiled. "Bless her, she loved children."

That rankled, because Daddy had said Mummy didn't love him, and he'd been a child once, so Susan loving kids was an outright lie.

Then he remembered Susan wasn't really Mummy, and he also remembered that time. *He relaxed, telling himself he didn't need to be upset about everything now, not when he knew the truth. But it was hard, so hard to switch his mind over from what his father had told him, what had been drummed into his head.*

"Yes, she loved children." Roland nodded. "I should go now. Back to my daughter. It's almost time to collect her from school."

"Oh, where does she go?"

Fuck. Bloody fuck. *"The little primary by my house. I really must go. Sorry for your loss." That last bit seemed an appropriate thing to say in the circumstances. The ladies of Jamaica Street had said the same.*

She nodded, patted his arm, and Roland pretended it was Mummy doing it. She dropped her hand to her side, and he walked away, trying not to go too fast in case that *seemed suspicious as well as his presence here.*

He left the cemetery, comforted to have felt her hand on him again. Soon, he'd meet Susan Gorman, and he'd feel even better.

* * *

Against the wall behind the cab of the artic stood a comfy armchair, which had spent most of its life in Jamaica Street, the only thing he'd taken from there. It had belonged to Mummy, given to her by her mother, a nan Roland couldn't remember. She'd died when he'd been three — he'd been told later: "The cancer got her, boy . . ." — and he sometimes wondered whether life would have been different had Nanny lived. Mummy might have eventually told her what Daddy was really like, and Nanny, she'd perhaps have urged her to leave him, taking Roland to a safer place.

But it hadn't turned out like that, and Roland had no choice but to get on with it.

He sat on the chair, stroking the arms that were covered in a floral-patterned fabric, the background once cream, now a fetching beige. The pink flowers he recalled from childhood were a dusky colour these days, the material wearing in places, frayed. Really, it was a sight, not something most people would keep, but it was the only thing left of his mother's, all her other things removed from the house once she wasn't in it anymore.

Daddy must have got rid of them while Roland was at school.

He looked across at the mummies. One day, when they'd completely decomposed, each bone dropping one after the other to form a pile on the floor, he'd box them up, keep them for licking, sucking them like lollipops. The decay process took years in the ground but less so out in the open, and some of their hair was still attached. It'd be a while before it disappeared, he'd read that in an internet café in Stroud.

The second mummy wasn't far off being the same as the first, and each one thereafter was in various stages of decomposition, right up to the freshest, Angela, beautiful lady, said so on her grave marker so it must be true. She didn't resemble Mummy, none of them did in reality, but in his mind he pretended they did, and that got him through.

The pole the hooks hung over was strong enough to hold around another five bodies, and he had the urge to add to his collection sooner than previous times. It was the obituary's fault, stating that Julieanne Lynch would be laid to rest today in Dullbourne Cemetery, closer to town, a bit dangerous for him perhaps, but he wanted to go there tonight just the same. And also Len Stobbart's fault, that butcher at the other end of the high street, the man who looked so much like Daddy, Roland didn't know why he hadn't chosen him over Dave.

People were entitled to make mistakes.

He had a shower, put on clean boxers, and went outside the artic and pulled down the ramp, watching the road from the corner of his eye. No traffic, and there wouldn't be. It was rarely used, a country lane on the outskirts, and no one would take any notice of an artic anyway. They were always parked up somewhere or other, weren't they, and it was assumed the driver had stopped for a nap. Driving while tired killed.

He reversed the Fiat out, put the ramp back, locked the lorry doors, then took a leisurely drive into town. He parked in the market square, lifting his hood, hiding his face. He paid the ticket fee, stuck the sticker in his car, then walked towards the butcher's. The rain was constant, puddles well-formed on the street, minimal shoppers, probably due to the storm that hadn't let up since it'd started last night.

Roland entered Stobbart's, shaking his arms to get rid of the rain on his puffa jacket, the droplets landing on the hardwearing bristly welcome mat just inside the door. Mr Stobbart was slicing breaded ham and stopped to peer at Roland, a broad smile fixed in place.

"Well, hello there. Come in for your lamb shank, have you?"

Roland liked a lamb shank. It reminded him of what it would be like to eat bits of raw Mummy so she was a part of him, always, his teeth grazing the bones. Stobbart sold them with a nice mint marinade all over them.

He was hungry. Daddy's testicles from last night were bound to be on their way through his colon by now. He'd eaten them with gusto, adding extra garlic, a second pinch of salt and pepper, and he'd even drizzled some sweet chilli sauce on the top.

Gourmet dining.

"Yes, a lamb shank, please. None of that frozen supermarket stuff for me. Fresh is best."

"It is that, sir. I've got a nice big one, just for you." Len took his gloves off, washed his hands at the sink beside the meat slicer, then dried them and put on fresh ones.

Len was very clean, did things the right way at work, just like Daddy.

While the butcher weighed the shank, Roland scoped out the shop, giving it more scrutiny now he knew he'd be back later. Len didn't have an assistant, he worked here by himself, the type of old-school businessman to close for lunch and damn the loss of profit. He always put a sign on the front door: BACK IN AN HOUR, FOLKS!

It had annoyed Roland something chronic at first, because an hour could mean anything without a specific time mentioned, but he'd discovered from keeping watch that it was between twelve and one, and Len was never a minute late in opening back up.

"There you go, my old fella." Len put the shank on the counter in a bag much like Dave's, except Stobbart's had a picture of a farm on it, various animals grazing by a fence, and the font was blue.

"Thanks." Roland paid. "I'll be seeing you later."

He left the shop, head down, a high-pitched giggle seeping out of him.

Oh yes, he'd be seeing him later all right.

CHAPTER SEVEN

Bethany didn't like the smell of raw meat, but here in Len Stobbart's shop, she had no choice but to breathe it in. The tang of fat was also present, churning her stomach.

They'd left Harold, the groundsman, feeling a little better than he had before they'd arrived at his little workplace, assuring him they'd be keeping an eye on the cemetery for a while after SOCO had gone. SOCO would be there for a day or so anyway, and hopefully, Bethany and Mike would have apprehended the killer by then. Harold could go to work without worrying, and life would trundle on.

She stood in front of the pristine glass counter showcasing its lamb and pork chops, the slabs of steak, the mince, the linked sausages, the tripe — *no, absolutely no* — and showed the man behind it her identification. "DI Bethany Smith and DS Mike Wilkins. We're here regarding Dave Johnson."

Stobbart's eyebrows hitched up, and he adjusted his white hat with the back of his blue-gloved hand. "What about him? What's he gone and done? To be honest, if you tell me he's in trouble with the law, I won't believe you."

"He's not in trouble, no."

A customer came in, and Stobbart served her a pound of lamb mince, for her shepherd's pie, she said. She left, grumbling about getting wet again, and the door snapped shut from the pull of the wind.

"Can we lock this for a moment?" Bethany asked. "The interruptions will hold us up if anyone else comes in, and we really need to crack on."

"Yep, you do that, and draw the blind down while you're at it. Customers know I do that when I nip out the back for a quick wee."

Lovely. Bethany snubbed the Yale then covered the door with the blue-and-white-striped blind. "Okay, sir, how did you get along with Dave?"

"Pretty well, considering we're so-called business rivals, but I never did hold with any of that rubbish. We both do well, so there's no need to be funny with each other, is there. In fact, I have a bevvy with him from time to time down at the Crow. He gave me a good tip about a new supplier actually. Just recently, it was. I have their first delivery tomorrow."

"Nice that you got along. Do you know of anyone who *didn't* get along with him?"

"Nah, he's a good old boy."

"Haven't you heard about what's happened?" she asked, curious because of his blasé manner and him not noticing her use of the past tense.

"Eh? I've been run off my feet as it happens. More customers than I can deal with earlier today, despite the weather being shitty. Haven't heard much except a long diatribe about Beryl's piles — she's my top customer, so it's best I let her ramble on."

Piles. Blimey. "The extra custom is maybe because Dave's is closed at the moment."

"Oh, is he ill? I'd have thought Owen would have opened up. He's almost at the end of his training so could cope by himself. That's one thing I need to do, get an assistant. The times I get sick, I can't work. Food, see. Could get contaminated with my germs."

"No, Owen can't do anything. Sadly, Dave was murdered last night."

"You bloody what?" The words came out as a shout. Stobbart's mouth hung open, and he grabbed the steel table in front of him for support. "That's knocked me for six, that has. Who'd want to murder him?"

"That's what we're trying to find out." She smiled. "So you don't know of anyone who'd do that?"

"No way." He shook his head. "How did they . . . ?"

"We're not disclosing that information at the minute, but I can confirm it was probably in his shop. Where were you last night?"

Stobbart blinked, staring at her as if her question was rude and had caught him off guard. "At home with the missus. We had the kids round for a bit of grub — well, they're not kids anymore, but you know what I mean. I took some chicken home and made a curry."

"Okay, we'll need their names, addresses, and your address so we can confirm that."

"It bloody well wasn't me!"

"I'm not saying it was, sir, it's standard procedure."

Stobbart gave the details, and Mike wrote them down.

"Do you have any customers who seem . . . strange at all in any way?" she enquired.

"What do you mean?" His forehead wrinkled.

"Abrupt, odd, anything that would raise a red flag."

Stobbart thought about that. "I've just had a fella in actually, a few minutes before you turned up." A knock sounded at the door. "Ignore that, probably Vera for her liver. She feeds it to the stray cats round her way. Back to the man. He always has a lamb shank, comes in quite often for it. Relatively new customer, only been around for about a month. He stares, which is a bit off-putting, and he always says: *Fresh is best.* Every single time. Like he's implying my produce *isn't* fresh. Can't explain why, but he's a bit peculiar. Gives off a funny vibe."

"What's his name?"

"No idea there, love, sorry." He paused. "So what's happening with young Owen then?"

"He's unable to go to work at the moment as Dave's shop is a potential crime scene, and until I find out from my team who Dave's next of kin is, there's no telling how long it'll be before the business is up and running again."

"Well, that's easy, the business will probably fold. The next of kin is Dave's ex-wife, he's leaving everything to her, and she won't want the bother of it. They parted on good terms, best friends. She's moved away, mind, to Wales I think he said. But she's the only person who'd need to know he's been kill . . . well, that he's gone. Nancy Johnson, if that helps."

"It does. They didn't have children?"

"Nah, that was the problem. She wanted them, he didn't. She stayed with him for nigh on thirty years, hoping, but Dave was too intent on running his shop to want nippers hanging off his leg when he got home. Dave's parents died years ago, and he was an only kid."

"That's been really helpful, thanks." She glanced at Mike.

He took his phone out and tapped the screen, getting hold of one of the team for her.

"Okay, we'll check your alibi — please don't worry, it really is just something we have to do — and if we need to speak to you again, we'll pop in." She rolled the blind up and unlocked the door.

"I'm really sorry to hear about Dave," Stobbart said.

"So are we." Bethany waved and stepped outside into the gale. It wasn't raining as much, so that was something, but she huddled under the flapping awning with Mike.

He showed her his phone from the top of the message conversation.

Mike: LOOK UP A NANCY JOHNSON IN THE WALES AREA. DAVE'S EX-WIFE.

Tammy: WILL DO. JUST TO LET YOU KNOW, WHEN I SPOKE TO HIM, OWEN

GIVENS MENTIONED A CUSTOMER WHO ALWAYS GIVES HIM THE CREEPS. GETS A STEAK EVERY TIME AND ALWAYS SAYS 'FRESH IS BEST'. THOUGHT I'D BETTER TELL YOU.

Mike: CHEERS, WE'LL GO TO SEE OWEN NOW THEN. IS HE AT HOME?

Tammy: HE WAS WHEN I PHONED HIM.

Mike: THANKS.

"Right, Owen's house it is, then we'll come back to look at Dave's shop," Bethany said.

They rushed to the car, walloped by a big gust, and she drove towards Owen's while they discussed the strange customer.

"While him saying 'fresh is best' is slightly unusual, especially *every* time he comes in, we really don't have anything to go on with this bloke," she said.

"Shall I message Leona, ask her to look at CCTV in the high street just before we went to Stobbart's?"

"Please. We might get lucky and spot the man, although what can we do if we manage to track him to a vehicle, run his plate, then find him? 'Oh, excuse me, sir, people have said you're bloody weird, so we think you might have killed a butcher and robbed a grave.'" She snorted. "Sorry, but we've still got nothing."

"I agree, but if we *do* find him, we can have a chat, suss him out."

"True. Can you also give her the details about Stobbart's kids and wife. Get her to send someone round there to check alibis. Uniform will do."

Mike sent the message, and she turned right into Owen's street.

"Leona's on it," Mike said.

"Fab. Come on then." She parked up. "Let's see what he has to say."

She ran up his path and rang the bell, turning her back to the rain that came at her in a slant. It tapped against her coat and hood. Mike joined her, and the door opened. A lad in his early twenties stood there, black hair, brown eyes, face haggard where he'd perhaps had little sleep from worrying.

She produced her ID and told him who they were. "We're here to talk about the customer, the one you mentioned to our colleague, Tammy Hill."

"Oh, come in." He stepped back, closing the door behind them.

Bethany eyed the cream carpet visible through the living room doorway and winced. "Shall we take our shoes off?"

"It's all right," Owen said. "Drops of rain won't hurt on the laminate out here, and the kitchen has lino, so we can go in there."

They followed him and sat around a mahogany table, Bethany decidedly soggy and uncomfortable from it.

"Okay, Owen, what's this about the man?" She smiled so he didn't think she was really here to arrest him, seeing as how Charlotte had said he was paranoid.

He shrugged. "It feels so stupid, bringing him up, but Miss Hill said to tell her about anyone weird *at all*, and he's the only weirdo I know. I actually *call* him Willy Weirdo. Not to his face, like, just to Dave. Look, he was worse than usual yesterday, said steak tasted better from a human but he'd have cow instead, something like that. *And* he asked me if I ate testicles."

"Pardon?" Bethany frowned, her stomach doing a somersault.

"Yeah, he said it'd make me manly because I'm a wimp."

"Excuse me just one moment. I need to make a phone call." Bethany left the room, closing the door, and stood at the foot of the stairs. She jabbed at her phone screen, shaking from that information. The man preferred human steak. *What?* "Isabelle, did you get a chance to have a proper look at every single body part yet?"

"Enough to know they're all present. I didn't get each piece out and examine them, though. Better that they remain in the bags to preserve any evidence."

"Right. Are they still there at the scene?"

"Yep, Presley's waiting for transportation to take them to the lab."

"Right. Can you have a look at the torso for me, specifically between where the legs would have been."

"Ah, do we have a sex-related crime on our hands or something? The case of the missing penis, dear Watson?"

"I'm not sure."

"Two secs." Isabelle's breathing and a grunt or two came down the line. "Oh, well, what do you know. No bollocks. His wedding tackle is still there, though. Blimey, how did you . . . ?"

"We're with Owen Givens. He mentioned a customer told him he enjoys human steak and asked him if he eats testicles, and I thought I'd take a punt and see if Dave's were present. Has any other part of him been sliced off, something he could use as steak?"

"I'll have a nose."

Bethany shuffled her feet while she waited.

"Not that I can see," Isabelle said. "At least you have a suspect now. Got a name?"

"If Willy Weirdo can be classed as one, yes. Listen, I have to go. See you soon." She returned to the kitchen and sat.

Mike tapped his notebook. "Owen was just saying that the weirdo hasn't been coming into the shop long."

The same as what Stobbart said. So, someone new around here? "Right. Does the shop have CCTV inside?"

"No." Owen fiddled with a hangnail that needed clipping off rather than pulling so it didn't bleed. "But I can tell you roundabout when he was in yesterday because I remember thinking, once he'd left, that I only had four hours to go before I could get off home. At that point, I didn't know Dave was going to let me go early, so that means I thought I'd finish at half five, so . . . yeah, that makes it about half one when the bloke was in."

She was pleased Mike was using his phone, probably to get Leona to look at yesterday's footage, too.

"That's fantastic info," she said. "Did Dave know him well?"

"No, he was just a customer. We get all sorts in, end up knowing their names an' all, but not his. Do you think he . . . he's the one who came to the shop and killed Dave?"

"We're following all lines of enquiry at the moment. Can you describe the man for us?"

"He's bald, got little dots of hair where it's growing though again, so I reckon he shaves it. Always wears a grey puffa jacket, black jeans. He's got a bogging face, and the skin round his mouth is red and sore."

"Sore?"

"Yeah."

"What do you mean by a 'bogging face'?"

Owen shrugged. "It's bloody odd. I can draw him if you want. I did art at school, the only thing I'm good at, but I still did crap in the exam." He got up and took a piece of A4 from a sideboard and a pencil from a drawer. Sitting, he got work.

Bethany and Mike remained seated while Owen drew, and Mike's phone bleeped. He leant across so she could see the screen.

> Leona: SENDING A PIC IN A SEC. SCREEN GRABS OF A FELLA ENTERING AND LEAVING STOBBART'S EARLIER. IT ISN'T MUCH GOOD TO US — HIS HEAD'S DOWN, AND HE'S GOT A HOOD UP — BUT WE CAN SEND IT TO THE TECHS TO DETERMINE HIS HEIGHT AND WEIGHT. I'LL LOOK FOR HIM GOING INTO DAVE'S EARLIER YESTERDAY IN A MO.
>
> Mike: THANKS.

The image popped up. He appeared tall, beefy, possibly strong — strong enough to wield a large cleaver and cut Dave to pieces. His clothing matched what Owen had said, so this was definitely him, but did he have anything to do with this? Was going after him a wild goose chase?

Owen had already drawn the outline of a wide face, a domed head. He was on the eyes now, which were rounded, as if the man was perpetually in shock. The eyebrows came next, thick, although a nice shape and not unruly at all. Maybe he plucked the outer edges. The nose appeared, Roman, large nostrils, big enough to fit a Maltester in each.

Mike's phone chirped.

Leona: SAME THING AT DAVE'S. HEAD BENT, FACE NOT IN VIEW AT ANY TIME. I ALSO CHECKED FROM FIVE UNTIL HALF PAST AGAIN, JUST TO MAKE SURE IT WASN'T MISSED BEFORE. HE DIDN'T ENTER THE SHOP FROM THE FRONT WHEN DAVE WAS MURDERED. NO ONE DID EXCEPT OWEN AND THEN GLEN AND TORY.

Mike: CHEERS, ME DEAR.

So whoever it was entered through the back.

"Owen, do you have to lock the gate when you leave work?" Bethany asked.

He continued drawing, the nose complete, the mouth almost done. "No. I park my car in the street behind, and Dave always padlocks the gate from the inside after I've arrived in the mornings then gone home at night. It was banging in the wind when I went out there, so he hadn't had a chance to do it."

Or he had, and someone climbed over to gain entry.

"Okay. What's round the back?" She'd have a look for herself in a bit when they visited the shop.

"Just an empty street."

Bethany stared at the A4. The mouth was fleshy. The man was downright ugly, stood out in a crowd, at least he would to her. The drawing was bloody good, though. Owen clearly had a flair for art, and she wondered how he could have done badly in his exam with work like that.

"That's as close to him as I can get," he said. "Some things are off, like his nose could do with being a bit slimmer, and I couldn't get the curve of his eyebrows right. In real life they're more like a woman's. Maybe he uses tweezers or whatever."

Just like she'd thought. "This is more than we had before we came to see you, so thank you very much. Of course, this man may not be anything to do with what happened to Dave, plenty of strange people around, but we'll look into him as much as we can. Have you ever noticed whether he gets into a car parked in the high street?"

"No."

A phone chirruped, and she didn't recognise it as hers or Mike's. Owen took his from his pocket and tapped the screen. He frowned.

"Bloody hell. Len Stobbart's offered me a job." He raised his head and stared at Bethany then Mike.

"That's brilliant. We did tell him you weren't able to work at the moment." A part of her wondered whether this had been Stobbart's plan all along, to kill Dave and nab Owen, but she dismissed it. His alibi would probably check out, and it was extreme to kill someone so you could nick their employee and bag all the business for yourself. *Is it, though?* No, it wasn't, people had killed for less, but Stobbart seemed genuine.

"It sounds weird, but I feel like I'm leaving Dave, even though I'm not." Owen rubbed his forehead and winced as though he had a headache.

"Not being funny, but as sad as this is," Mike said, "life still goes on, and you have a living to make. Take the job."

Owen nodded. "He said to come at eight tomorrow morning."

"Right, we'll leave you be for now." Bethany rose. "If we need to chat again, we'll get hold of you." She picked up the picture. "And thanks for this, much appreciated. If you remember anything else, give me a ring." She dropped her card on the table then put the image inside her jacket.

Mike got up, and they left Owen in peace, rushing to the car, getting drenched now the rain was coming down harder. Bethany took the A4 out and placed it on the dash. They slid their seat belts on, and Mike received another message.

"Dave's ex-wife's been found," he said. "Leona's dealing with telling the police in Laugharne. Dylan Thomas lived there, did you know that?"

"Nope. Who is he?"

"An author."

"You know some random shit. Okay, ask Leona if they can arrange for his ex to come here if she's aware she's down as his next of kin. That shop will need dealing with by someone, plus his funeral once his body parts are released."

Mike sent the message.

She took a picture of the image Owen had drawn and sent it to Rob and Fran so it could be distributed to officers.

"Are we going to Dave's shop now?" Mike asked.

"Yep, then to see that other butcher. It'll probably be a waste of time, but it's best to tick all the boxes."

The problem was, there weren't any ticks in those boxes, just crosses, dead ends. If Dave's killer wasn't the strange man, who the hell was it?

CHAPTER EIGHT

SOCO milled around in Dave's shop, and Bethany, kitted up, walked around to get a feel for the place. She stood where Dave would have behind the counter, unable to see into the street as blinds covered the window and door. Needing an idea of the view, she went outside. Opposite was a gym, and either side of that a New Look and a Salvation Army charity shop.

Uniform had already been into those plus the other shops, asking if people had seen anything early yesterday evening. No one had. CCTV hadn't shown anyone in the high street at that time anyway, and all businesses reported a complete lack of customers from about ten to five onwards, Mother Nature having kept them at home. Employees had left from the rear exits, so an empty street was all they'd had until Owen and the odd punter up the other end entered the Crow. All faces were visible, and no one had a grey puffa jacket or black jeans.

Bethany put fresh booties on and went inside. Mike was out the back, so she joined him and studied the meat-cutting area. Ahead, a steel table. The magnet wall strip. Floor-to-ceiling white tiles. The hook the saw had hung on. The messy hose. To the right of all that, two doors. One led into the yard, the other she wasn't sure of yet.

"Shall we have a gander in there?" Mike pointed to the unidentified door. "It's the meat room."

She shrugged. "May as well."

They entered, and she really should have just stayed away. The smell . . . And seeing all the hanging carcases was disturbing, bringing it home that the chops or steaks she associated with dinner came off these bodies. She wandered between each one, checking the floor, despite knowing SOCO had already done so. Next, she inspected the animals, but nothing seemed out of place.

Until she spotted what looked like a red brand on the leg of one.

"What do you make of that?" She gestured to it, unwilling to go down on her haunches to see what it said. "Something the farmers put on there?"

Mike came closer and crouched. "I doubt a farmer would put 'Be Manly!' on a bloody cow."

Her stomach lurched. *What?* "Owen mentioned something about being manly. That bloke said it to him, to do with the testicles." She examined it some more. "That's a red marker, don't you think? Someone just wrote it on the fat rind." She opened the door and called out, "Did anyone clock this in here or what?"

A SOCO came over. "What's that?"

She pointed to the cow's leg.

"Oh, yeah. Strange, isn't it? Photos have been taken." He walked out, his hand held up in a wave.

"So we *are* looking for that bloke then," she said to Mike. "Too much of a coincidence for it to not be him."

"It appears so. I checked my phone while you were in the high street just now. Leona messaged to say there's no CCTV out the back. All the cameras are concentrated in the shopping area, so she can't check for vehicles leaving from the rear or even where they could have gone, not until the cams start on the A road out of Shadwell. She's got a couple of officers on it with her so they can get a list of cars when they hit the first outbound camera, but it's going to take a while without a number plate to go on."

"So we have no idea whether he came here in a vehicle or on foot last night, although if he carted a body away, he'd need a car."

"She said that during the day when he went to Stobbart's, he parked in the market square and walked to the shop, but unfortunately, he had his hood up, and the way the camera's angled, only the top corner of his vehicle roof is visible. She said it could be any number of makes."

"The market square parking metre issues tickets without drivers having to input their plates, so we're shit out of luck there. I assume Leona's also going to be checking all the cameras that would've picked up his car before he parked in the square."

"She's on that now."

"Right, I'll message Fran with a picture of this leg." She used her phone to snap a couple of images, zooming so she didn't have to get up close and personal. She sent them off with an explanation.

Fran: SO WE ASSUME HE DID THAT AFTER HE KILLED DAVE?

Bethany: OR MAYBE HE WENT IN THE MEAT ROOM TO HIDE BEFOREHAND AND WROTE IT THEN.

Fran: GOD, HE COULD EVEN HAVE BEEN IN THERE AT THE TIME OWEN LEFT.

Bethany: BLOODY HELL. IF SO, OWEN HAD A CLOSE SHAVE.

She put her phone in her pocket, and as they left the meat room, she spotted a shelf with various knickknacks opposite. Owen had mentioned taking his phone off a shelf, so this must be it. On there was a red marker.

"Bag this, please," she called, thinking of fingerprints.

A SOCO came and collected it.

"I assume it was used to write on the cow's leg, so get that sent off ASAP."

They inspected the yard next. The padlock on the gate was secure, as Owen had sorted that last night, and nothing untoward lurked beneath the outdoor display fridge or the tarpaulin over it in the covered area. She imagined someone scaling the gate, easily slipping inside the building, then turning left and entering the meat room to hide, waiting for Owen to leave.

Back in the main part of the shop, she was saddened by some minced beef out on the counter, some bags beside it as if Dave had been in the middle of packing it up to put away. SOCO had said the blinds were down when they'd entered, so had Dave decided to close early? Or had the killer lowered them so no one in the gym or the shops would spot him?

"We'd better go and see the other butcher," she said to Mike, who frowned at Dave's phone beside the weighing machine.

"What's that still doing here?" He shook his head. "Digi could have had a good nose through that by now." He went out the back to have a word with an officer about sending it to the station, then called Bethany. "We need to look in the street behind."

"Better off going in the car so we don't touch that padlock on the gate."

They left the shop after taking off their protective clothing and popping it into an evidence bag, which they handed to a SOCO. She drove to the rear of the shop, and like Owen had said, it was an empty road. Scrubland went back for a mile or so, then some homes on the edge of a housing estate.

"Get hold of Rob for me, will you? Uniform can go and question the people in those houses," she said. "Not that they'd have seen anything from that far away, but I'd rather it was done."

She drove back around to the shopping centre while Mike did that, parking as close to it as she could in the new multi-storey. They walked through into the precinct, and Volton's sat between a GAP and a Home Bargains. The butcher's was a large shop with several workers, the right-hand side for meat with a long counter, the left with freezers containing things to go with it — chips, peas, apple pies, sausage meat and the like. Shelving above held sauces, marinades, everything you'd need to create a good stew or curry, and a few more meals besides.

Bethany approached the counter and asked for Thomas Volton.

"That man there." A spotty lad pointed to an older gentleman with brown hair packaging what looked like lamb cutlets.

She smiled. "Thank you."

Mr Volton turned at that moment, and she raised a hand and beckoned him. He came over, taking off his gloves, and she leant across so only he could hear her.

"DI Bethany Smith and DS Mike Wilkins. If you'd rather I show you my ID somewhere private . . ."

His thin eyebrows arched, and he nodded. "Let's go to my office out the back."

She walked to a door at the rear and followed him through, Mike behind her. A meat-cutting area similar to Dave's met her, except there were three steel tables and a lot more implements. Volton continued on to another door. Through there was a short hallway with a door either side, both with plaques: OFFICE. STAFFROOM.

In the office, Volton sat at a grey desk covered in invoices, notepads, and a diary. An empty coffee cup sat on a coaster with cow print on it.

Bethany showed him her ID. "We're here about Dave Johnson. Have you heard?"

"What I've heard is he's closed shop. Plenty of customers coming in here today grumbling about it. *I'm* not grumbling, though." Volton chuckled and drummed his fingers on a stack of paper, the top sheet curling in one corner. "He's changed suppliers, apparently, and I did wonder if the goods weren't up to snuff. Maybe that's why he had to shut down."

"No, that's fine as far as I know. How did you get along with him?"

Volton laughed. "How does the manager of Sainsbury's get on with the one at Tesco? The answer is, they probably don't know each other, and if they do, they're not going to go round in a strop with one another over a job, because that's all it is. Two men working in similar places."

"Did you know him?"

"No, only of him. Heard he's a nice man. There's a need for three butchers in Shadwell, so it's pointless being rivals. It's like books. Loads of writers and loads of people needing what they're putting out. Enough to go round, something for all tastes. Dave's more your traditional butcher, though — limited pre-packed goods, mainly sausages and burgers. As you probably saw, I'm traditional plus commercial. I cater to people who want their food weighed, plus those in a rush who haven't got time to queue and just want to grab a packet of mince for their spag bol and go home. I've got everything in here they'll need to make their dinner, and it saves them queuing in the supermarkets."

"That makes sense." She took a deep breath, really not needing his long explanation. "This might come off as a weird question, but bear with me. Do you know of anyone who'd want to harm Dave?"

"No clue. As I said, I know *of* him. Volton's is a chain — I have shops up and down the country. I'm too busy to worry about what someone else is up to, if you catch my drift. I mind my own business, figuratively and literally."

"Have you noticed anyone, let's say a tall, well-built man in a grey puffa jacket and black jeans, hanging around outside your shop, maybe even coming in?" She took her phone out and accessed the picture Owen had drawn. "Someone a bit like this?"

Volton took her mobile and peered at it. "Blimey, you wouldn't miss him at a fancy-dress party, would you.

Hunchback of Notre Dame. Talk about falling out of the ugly tree and hitting every branch on the way down. Now you're going to make me feel a bastard and tell me he's got a condition, aren't you?" He handed the phone back.

"Perhaps he has. So, does he ring any bells?"

Volton all but wet himself, and she cursed what she'd said. Mike coughed a few times.

Volton composed himself. "That was funny. I like your wit. I can't say I've seen him, no, but one of my employees may have. Feel free to ask them." He paused, then, "You mentioned someone harming Dave. Was he robbed or something? Only asking so I know to be more vigilant. Mind you, with security here, I'd say we're safer."

"He was murdered yesterday evening, around closing time."

Volton's eyes widened, but that was the only tell that he was alarmed. "It was a ghost town about then, what with the weather. Opportunist thieves, was it?"

"Nothing was taken from the shop as far as we're aware."

"That doesn't make sense."

"No, which is why we need to know of anyone who's holding a grudge."

"I wouldn't know." He stood. "Let's see if one of the lads recognises that man, shall we?"

"I think you need to take precautions," Bethany said. "Maybe go somewhere until all this has died down. I don't feel you're safe. At the very least, we could offer you some police protection."

"Nah, you're all right, but thanks for your concern. You lot have got enough to do, let alone babysitting me."

He led the way out, effectively ending the interview. She should be annoyed or even curious about it, but he was clearly the type to know when meetings had reached their terminus — and that he didn't care much about Dave, alive or dead. It could be said that made him heartless, but regardless, she'd bet he was no killer.

In the shop, she showed each employee the image, and only one had seen him, about three weeks ago.

"He'd come in asking for . . ." The blond thirty-something man cleared his throat, his cheeks going red. "Testicles. I told him we didn't sell them, and he stared at me, for ages like, then said, 'Try them. They'll make you manly.' He walked out, and I haven't seen him since."

What was this 'manly' shit about? Were they looking for someone who'd been emasculated and felt the need to become more masculine? What did eating testicles have to do with that? Was it from the saying about growing a pair of balls, and he'd gone one step farther down the road of nuttiness by consuming them?

Christ . . .

"Okay, what was he wearing that day?" Mike asked.

"Grey coat. Can't remember the rest." He shrugged.

"And what time was that?" Bethany shivered from the cold draught coming from the counter.

"In the afternoon, no idea when. I just know it was past lunch. Hang on, after school, because a fair few kiddies were around."

"Do you have CCTV in here?"

"No, but the shopping centre area does, you know, out there." He pointed to the covered walkway in front of the shops. "You might catch him coming in and going out, but then I don't even remember which day it was, so that's a lot of CCTV to watch."

"That's fine. So let me get this straight. He came in, said what he said, and didn't buy anything?"

"Nope. I just assumed because we didn't have what he wanted, he'd try somewhere else, although I don't know anywhere that sells those."

"Thanks."

They left the shop and eventually found the offices for the shopping centre after following some signs fashioned to resemble those you get on nature walks — a pole with black cast-iron arrows on the top, gold lettering. They had to take a lift to the second floor, and a receptionist sat behind a glass desk and directed them to the CCTV room once she'd seen Bethany's ID. They spoke to a couple of men who lounged in front of a bank of monitors, and on shelves, loads of small TVs.

"Sorry, that footage is gone. We keep each week for the following week," the black-haired one said.

Shit. "Do you watch the screens all day?"

"Yep, then if there's any trouble, we radio down to security who are in the precinct."

"This might be a long shot, but have you seen a man who looks like this, probably hanging around outside Volton's?" She got the picture up on her phone. "Grey puffa jacket, black jeans."

Black Hair nudged his colleague. "Oi, that's the weirdo, isn't it?"

Bethany's heart leapt.

"Which weirdo?" The blond frowned. "There are so many of the buggers."

"*The* weirdo." Black Hair sighed. "You know, the one Noel had to have a word with a while back. I think it was Noel anyway. Don't you remember? He was sitting on one of the benches outside the butcher's playing with those rubber testicles."

"Oh, *him.*" Blond studied the image. "Yeah, that's the bloke all right. You can't miss his mug."

Bethany felt a tad sick. "Testicles?"

Blond nodded. "They were made of that squidgy stuff. Stress balls, literally. He was squeezing and sniffing them."

"Okay . . ." Bethany swallowed.

Mike turned away to face the door, his shoulders shaking.

Black Hair laughed. "We've seen some strange things, but that was the oddest for me. Sandra, the balloon lady, it was her who called it in. Every shopkeeper or stall worker has a radio, see, and one of the channels comes directly to us. So we got him on camera, and plain as day, he's sniffing them."

"I didn't see a balloon lady," Bethany said.

"She's normally got her little cart thing outside Volton's," Blond said. "Sells birthday cards an' all, and small teddies. She's off sick today, though. She said he was muttering about his mum, saying she was a bitch but not a bitch. Buggered if I know what that's all about."

"What happened regarding the incident?" Bethany asked.

"He was asked to refrain from doing what he was doing, and to stop using profanity, or he had to leave." Black Hair consulted a ledger, which he flipped through. "Here we are, it *was* Noel who dealt with it." He checked the many monitors. "And he's outside B&M now. Want me to radio him to let him know you need a chat?"

"Please. Thanks for your help. The info's really useful."

They took the lift down to the shopping area and walked to B&M. Noel came over to them when she held her ID up, and he confirmed what the CCTV men had said.

"It wasn't so much the weird things he was fiddling with," Noel said, "because you couldn't make out what they were anyway. I only knew because I asked him to show me. You can't be too careful these days, can you, especially in a shopping centre. It was the swearing that bothered me. Kids hang about the balloon stall, and we wouldn't want them hearing him effing and blinding."

"How did he seem to you?"

"Agitated. Annoyed. Jittery at first, then his expression switched — that was creepy, I can tell you. It went from scrunched up to nothing. I couldn't read what he was thinking then at all. He left the centre via the doors that lead to the multi-storey."

"What about CCTV there?"

"Same policy as in here. It's gone after a week."

"When you say jittery . . ."

"Well, I asked him to pack it in with the swearing, and he said bitch wasn't a swear word because that's a female dog. To be honest, that's the sort of rubbish you expect to hear from a cocky teenager, not a grown bloke. I told him no matter what the word was, he needed to stop or leave. If he continued, he faced a ban. That's when he got up, sniffed those things he was holding — right in my face, he did it — and walked away. I followed to make sure he was going, plus I remained by the exit for a while. I got hold of CCTV to keep an eye on all exits in case he came back. He didn't. I haven't seen him since."

Bethany reckoned the killer had probably abandoned doing anything to Volton because he'd get spotted here easily — and recognised. So he'd chosen Dave, for whatever reason, and that left Len Stobbart as vulnerable if butchers were the target.

They returned to the car. She drove to Stobbart's, nipped in, and warned him to be vigilant, careful, now she knew their man had visited all the butchers. He said he was working late to do his books but would make sure he locked himself in.

Back in the driver's seat, she sent a message to Fran.

Bethany: ANY NEWS YET?

Fran: WE'RE ALL STILL WORKING ON THINGS. I'VE HAD A CHANCE TO LOOK AT SOCIAL MEDIA QUICKLY, JUST NOT IN DEPTH YET. ONLY THOMAS VOLTON HAS A BUSINESS PAGE ON FACEBOOK, BUT NOT A PERSONAL ACCOUNT. TWITTER IS THE SAME. IT'S MAINLY DEALS OF THE DAY, RECIPES, STUFF LIKE THAT.

Bethany: OKAY, IF NOTHING ELSE COMES IN BEFOREHAND, FINISH AT YOUR USUAL TIME. TOMORROW IS ANOTHER DAY.

She turned to Mike. "Fancy dinner in the Flapping Crow?"

"Now how the bloody hell did I know you were going to say that?"

She laughed. "Bugger it. I'm becoming predictable."

CHAPTER NINE

Roland arrived at Dullbourne Cemetery, parking his car round the back of the church. No groundsman here like at Wallflower, but the vicar had locked up a while ago, shuffling away with his head bent, down the sloping path and disappearing into the darkness of early evening, the last sight Roland had of him the fluttering of his white robe. The vicar lived a few streets away — Roland had followed him several times, so he should know — and there wouldn't be any trouble from that quarter.

No one had braved the elements in over two hours to place flowers on graves — he'd stood and observed behind a cedar tree, which he'd stroked and hugged while he was at it. What would be the point of people visiting here anyway? They'd be blown away in this horrible weather. While the rain had let up, the wind hadn't, but at least he'd stay dry for now.

He collected his big shovel, his rope ladder, and, hood up, chin to chest, walked down the grassy aisles between graves, looking for the one belonging to Julieanne Lynch while at the same time ensuring no stray mourners had escaped his notice.

Ah, there it was, right at the back, probably because there was limited space here now. It was easily identified in the murk by the mounds of light-coloured flowers either side — she must have been loved, just like Mummy. Although Daddy hadn't loved her once she'd gone, Roland still had, hating her in equal measure.

He strode over to it and wondered who all the people were who'd left the blooms for his mother. It was sad that he didn't know. She must have made a great many friends since—

Stop that. She didn't make new friends. It isn't her in the ground.

He knew that, of course he did, he just sometimes got a bit confused.

A lot confused.

A quick glance around showed there was definitely no one about, so he got to work, moving the flowers away from one side to give him space to pile the mud. Time passed. His big spade and the earth being loose, albeit wet, meant he'd only used a couple of his precious hours to dig. He needed to get a move on if he was going to kill Daddy again later. The butcher always stayed behind on this night of the week. Roland had spied through the back windows three times and observed him doing his paperwork at a desk, a white lamp with a curved neck giving off limited light.

He secured his rope ladder by its hooks in the grass beneath the line of wreaths, where the earth was still packed tight. In his pocket he had a heavy lever, and it was always touch and go as to whether he could prise the coffin lid off without a struggle. Down in the hole, he straddled the pine box — or it might be oak, he didn't give much of a shit — and wedged his lever beneath the lid. He leant on it with both gloved hands, pouring his body weight onto it. The lid creaked then snapped up, almost bashing him in the face, and he took it off, propping it at the top end.

He switched his phone torch on and aimed the beam at her.

There she was, Mummy, all pale skin and russet hair; she must have dyed it at some point. She had a pretty dress on, pink silk, nothing like she'd have chosen years ago, and he reckoned someone else had picked it, sending her off to Heaven in clothes she wouldn't be seen dead in.

Hahaha.

There were a few items in there with her. A plastic red rose, a doll — perhaps from her childhood it was that ratty, its face scuffed on one cheek and one eye shut, the other staring at him accusingly — and a letter in a peach-coloured envelope. Who the hell had written to her? How come they got to send her notes and he didn't? He stuffed it in his pocket and got down to the business of getting her out.

She draped nicely over his shoulder, and he hauled her up the ladder, huffing and puffing, having to dump her on the flowers, squashing them. That was a pest, and someone would see they'd been wrecked — his fault for not moving them *all* away. He went back down to put the lid on, collected his lever, which he put back in his pocket with his phone, then climbed out to stand beside her, ruining a nice bunch of lilies beneath his big boots.

The moon came out from behind a storm cloud, giving the area some light. Her head rested on the U of a MUM wreath, and that got him a little irate. So she'd had other children when she'd left? Had cared for them and not him? She must have for someone to put that there.

He kicked her in the head for being so insensitive, so rude, and it was Mummy's cheek he bent over and slapped, not Julieanne's. She *was* a bitch after all, like Daddy had always told him.

No, she wasn't. You know she wasn't.

Do I believe Daddy?

No, the Enlightenment told the truth.

He grabbed her roughly, a carnation snagging in her hair, and carried her to his car, glancing everywhere for anyone coming his way.

No one about.

The majority of her folded into the boot well enough with a bit of persuasion, but her left leg was being annoying the way it wouldn't bend, so he broke the fucking thing.

"That'll teach you."

He shut the lid and ran back to the grave. Replaced three quarters of the mud. Moved the crushed flowers so they were beneath the ones he hadn't ruined. Put the rest back down the other side. Then he got in the car and drove away, so excited to lick Mummy's cheek once he got her to the artic.

With his headlights doused, he pulled into the yard at Stobbart's with the engine off.

He needed to be careful. While the high street was pretty empty when he'd driven past the top end to come here, there were a few people smoking outside the pub. Stobbart's was three shops down from there, so if the bloke made a racket, someone might hear.

That's if he's even there. Maybe I'll get a lucky break.

The butcher wasn't at his desk, but the lamp was on, highlighting a ledger and a stack of what could be till receipts. Good man, doing his paperwork weekly, probably so his accountant had an easier job.

Roland took a new plastic poncho out of the glove box and put it on over his jacket, drawing the hood up. He grabbed his roll of sturdy black bags, got out, and slid his lever from his pocket. Tried the back door, which was locked, so jimmied it, cringing at the cracking sound but pleased the wood hadn't splintered. No one would know he'd broken in just by looking at it.

He waited — one beat, two, three and then four — for Stobbart to come running, but . . . nothing. Then Roland was inside, the lever still gripped tight in his gloved hand, and he crept past the office, through the meat-cutting area, where he placed his black bags on the steel table. In the doorway at the rear of the shop, he stared.

Stobbart was on his knees, his back to Roland. He had those over-the-ear headphones on that people used in the gym over the road from Dave's. Bright yellow, they were, curved rubber snakes stuck to the skin behind his red ears. He was chalking a picture of a leg of lamb on a blackboard, having already written the words: BUY ONE, GET ONE FREE! SHANKS A MILLION FOR YOUR CUSTOM!

That got Roland's goat. How discourteous was it to offer other people the chance to have a free minted lamb shank? *Two* of them for the price of one? Stobbart had only given him one earlier, and what a scam that was if he knew damn well tomorrow there was a special offer on.

Roland stuffed his thumb in his mouth, the leather of his glove cold on his tongue.

Stobbart sang, the sudden out-of-tune words giving Roland a jolt. Something about dancing in the moonlight. Well, he'd be doing the dance of death in a minute, but the moon wasn't here to watch. It hid behind the blinds at the window and door, as did the rain, which pattered on the glass at a steady rate.

Roland was going to get all muddy again when he buried Daddy.

He popped his thumb out, raised the lever, sharp end pointed downwards, and tiptoed up behind the butcher. It was his father all over again, a working man who was nice to the customers but cruel to his son — the BOGOF proved that. Images from the past flickered through his mind, and he stopped walking and arced the lever down. It dug right into the back of the man's neck as though it belonged there, quite at home, thank you. Stobbart screamed, and Roland clamped his left hand over that gaping mouth, tugging him up on his feet, his back flush to Roland's front.

He held him tight so he could wrench the lever free, blood escaping, then curled his arm around and stabbed the fucker in the guts. Again, again, again. With each strike, Stobbart groaned behind the hand, and Roland couldn't blame him. The lever wouldn't go in as smoothly, as gloriously as a knife. No, it'd hurt, a crippling stab and a punch at the same time. Double whammy, this is for Mammy.

The butcher sagged, sliding to his knees. Roland let him go, and Daddy rolled onto his back, clutching his stomach. Blood oozed between his sausage fingers — fitting that he had those — soaking into his blue T-shirt, a cartoon family on the front, probably those Simpson people, seeing as everyone was yellow.

Blood bubbled out of his mouth, and his lips moved as if he said something. His teeth, tinged with red, reminded Roland of watching *Dracula* recently on his phone. He couldn't hear anything that made sense, but he imagined Daddy said, "Be manly, boy!" and "Come here and lick my . . ."

"Shut up," Roland snarled. "Shut up right now."

He kicked Daddy in the head, just the same as he'd done to Mummy at the grave, so that was the pair of them with a throbbing temple now, although she'd no longer be feeling the pain. Then he slapped *his* cheek, too, once, twice, and the pitiful man wailed.

"Why are you doing this to me?" Tears tracked down onto Daddy's earbuds, and he moaned.

Roland ripped those little sods out so he could be heard. Tinny music came out of them, and he recognised the melody. *I've Got You Under My Skin* by that Sinatra fella. He threw them to one side. "You know why. Don't pretend you don't." He stared at the lever in his fist. Blood dripped onto the floor tiles, creating a circle of splodges. "Hurting, is it?"

"P-please. Call an ambulance. T-take the money in the safe. The combination's seven-four-one-five. I won't tell anyone."

"You sound like those pathetic people in books and films. *Please, I'll keep this a secret. No one will know. I'll never tell them who you are.*"

"I swear, I'll say . . . someone came in . . . and robbed me . . . but I . . . ouch . . . but I didn't . . . see your face."

"Why would I rob you? I have enough money of my own, but thanks for the offer. I'm not a *thief*, for God's sake."

But you are. A thief of life.

That doesn't count.

"W-what . . . are . . ." Daddy's voice was getting weaker. "You . . . going . . . to—"

"Do to you?" Roland tilted his head. "You want to *know*?"

Daddy nodded.

Fool.

"What a sick individual you are." Roland let out that high-pitched giggle of his. "Let me tell you a story then. I'm going to strangle you in a minute. You'll feel like your lungs are going to pop from lack of air. I bet your eyes will hurt an' all, bulging, straining, and in the end, I imagine you'll just black out. It'll be a mercy, because I could do the next bit while you're still alive, but you and I know what a mess that'll make."

Why wasn't this prat getting up, trying to run away?

"Oh God . . ." Daddy jerked, possibly from a fresh slice of pain.

"God? Him? He'll turn you away and send you to the Devil." Roland paused. "But we're getting ahead of ourselves. Let's get back to the story. After all, you like telling those, too. Once you're dead, I'll have a cup of tea if you have any left, considering you drink so much of it throughout the day. Three sugars — I know you don't use sweetener. And full-fat milk, a man after my own heart. I don't enjoy that green-top rubbish either. I'll go and visit your meat locker, leave a little message in there, and then I'll make a second drink. I need to waste time, much as I don't like it. Perhaps half an hour, three quarters. Not so much blood spilling when I lop your arms and legs off then. It congeals after death, as you know. Looks a bit like that bum jam. Did you hear about that? Some bloke sliced people's arse cheeks off and made jam out of the flesh. Clever. Happened right here in Shadwell, so you must have read the news. I saw it on telly when I was back in Jamaica Street. *Jam*-aica. Ha."

Daddy either didn't get the joke or wasn't finding it funny.

What a bastard.

Pools of red covered the tiles either side of him now, and behind his neck. Roland got upset with himself for doing something that had created a mess. He'd always strangled before, but this time, that free lamb shank business had brought on a red mist, and here they were. He just had to hope the hose reached this far. Dave's would have, but this wasn't Dave's shop, was it. Maybe buckets of water and a broom were in his future. There was no question of leaving it like this. Daddy had taught him that you never left blood at the end of the shift. Roland had spent many a time after school helping out in the shop, and when he was older, working there during the day. He'd learnt so much. Something to be grateful to him for, he supposed.

"My wife," Daddy burbled. "My kids."

"You only have one child."

The butcher frowned. "W-what? I have two, a boy and a girl."

"No, you just have one." Roland glared. "Me."

"I-I don't get it. What are you *talking* about?" Stobbart slumped, closed his eyes.

Ah, he was getting tired. All that unfortunate blood loss.

Roland stepped around the spillage and went behind him. He knelt and lifted the wretched man so his shoulders rested on Roland's knees, blood from his neck smearing the poncho. Roland clasped his hands around his neck, the gloves giving him a fantastic grip.

And he squeezed.

It didn't take long for the king of pigs to go limp. He'd hardly struggled; such a pleasant passing compared to the others. Roland dragged him out to the cutting area and lifted him, glad of the poncho so his jacket didn't get dirty. He slung the body on the steel table and set about undressing him, a disgusting task, but it wasn't as if anyone else was here to lend him a hand, was it?

With the clothes in a black bag in the office — he pulled the blinds down in there while he was at it — he moved to the little kitchen and made himself the tea. The cup had a yellow person on it as well, so Daddy must have got into watching the show at some point.

It isn't Daddy.

While he drank, he accessed the phone that had been in the trouser pocket. Spotify was on, so he pressed STOP and closed the app, then had a good nose through the image folder, incensed at pictures of the butcher with a woman — nothing like Mummy, so Daddy must have been having a secret affair — and two other people. Those kids he mentioned? They appeared younger than Roland by about five years, so yes, definitely a secret life, a new family tucked away all this time, Roland knowing nothing about it until now.

That hurt.

Why did Daddy have to lie so much?

With all the pictures inspected, his tea finished, he took a blue marker from a mug on the office desk and entered the meat room. This part always frightened him. Reminded him of—

Just get on with it.

He held his breath and chose a lamb, wanting to make a point about the free shank malarkey, and wrote a message for the police. If they even found it. He'd done this at Dave's before he'd killed him, had run out to hide when the butcher had come to investigate the noise Roland had made. He'd hit the wall with his lever, angry at the past and what had happened in the meat room, forgetting for a moment that Dave was around and would hear him.

He'd thought of himself as not stupid, but in that moment, he was.

"Don't be stupid again."

He jammed the marker up a pig's nostril and left the room.

The act of making another cuppa soothed his ragged nerves, slowed his manic breathing, and he let excitement take over — excitement about cutting those testicles off and eating them later. His mouth watered at the thought of the garlic, the salt and pepper, and instead of sweet chilli sauce, he reckoned he'd give HP a go. That'd spice it up a bit.

He drank, keeping an eye on the time, and when his cup was empty, he washed it in hot water, Fairy, and bleach, giving it a good scrub with the green abrasive side of a sponge. It wasn't quite the moment yet, so he checked the hose for length, tugging it out into the shop. Oh, there was enough, so he switched the water on and washed the back of the door and the blind, the frame, and the wall where blood had splashed when he'd stabbed Daddy in the stomach. He pointed the spray at the mud from his boots and the blood on the floor in the direction of the gap between the counter and the window. He didn't need pink liquid seeping under the front door, although it was raining, so it would get washed away. But still . . .

He followed the diluted blood as it whooshed behind the counter, jetting it along and into the cutting area. It swirled down the drain in the floor, just like in his artic. Water turned off, he returned to the shop with a long-poled squeegee and pushed the remaining wetness over the grate. Apart from a pink stain or two on the blind, you wouldn't know someone had been killed in here.

Perfect.

And here it was. *That* moment.

He chose a small knife and opened Daddy's legs. Those yummy testicles hung low within wrinkled sacs, hairs sparse and thin, and he held the fat sausage up while he sliced into the skin beneath, around the base. He peeled the skin back and cut the balls free, and they plopped onto the table with a rewarding thud.

Roland used one of the shop's meat bags to put them in, knotted the top, and popped them in his pocket. They were beside his own balls, warm, so he was twice as manly now.

Next, he selected the largest cleaver, one sharp enough to go through bone, and busied himself doing what had to be done. He worked swiftly, black-bagging the body parts as he always did, trekking each package into the office, two at a time.

He used the hose again, cleaning his boots, too, then sorted the special sanitiser and scrubbing brush, and soon the cutting area gleamed, and the shop floor shone with dampness where he'd mopped it. He washed the knife and cleaver, replaced them on the wire mesh rack on the wall above the table. Dave had been much more sensible in having the magnetic strip.

Satisfied all was in order, he hefted the bags onto the back seat of his car, clothes an' all — there was no way Daddy would fit in the boot with Mummy — and he drove away, using the road without any cameras. He arrived at Dullbourne Cemetery, not worried this time about anyone spotting him. Most people would be tucked up in their beds by now.

Lucky me.

CHAPTER TEN

Roland blinked, his eyes stinging. That got him into trouble, crying. It wasn't manly to do that. The thing was, he wasn't a man, so of course he was going to cry, especially when Daddy did that.

Years had passed like this, no one out there for him to turn to, no one who even seemed to care what was going on inside the little house in Jamaica Street. The women neighbours, some of them had moved on, and even though others remained, because Daddy was so nice and kind, they didn't suspect anything.

"Just stay there like that," Daddy said.

Roland wasn't going to move — couldn't anyway. Being pinned saw to that. He was facedown on the floor, the coarse carpet itching his skin, and Daddy licked his back. Roland would have to do it to him in a minute, and while he hated it, dreaded it, at the same time it comforted him.

He'd stopped questioning his higgledy-piggledy feelings long ago.

Now, though, things were changing. Roland had noticed girls, and with his teenage years just around the corner, he wanted someone to kiss, someone to cuddle. He could pretend it was Mummy then, especially if they had boobs. He vaguely remembered what that felt like, a soft fleshy pillow beneath his cheek, her steady heartbeat thudding away under his ear, her hand stroking his hair.

He wanted a girl so he could lick her skin.

"Your turn," Daddy said.

For a while, Roland had wanted to call him Dad, like other kids did to theirs, but it wasn't allowed. Once, when he'd been dropped off at school one morning, he'd called him Dad and got told off for it, was forced to say it 'properly', and another boy had heard him.

Bullies weren't nice people.

Roland did what he had to, and now it was all over, Daddy told him to go out and mow the grass. The sun had been relentless all day, baking everyone in the classrooms, and although it was close to dinner-time, it was too warm for mowing. Still, he'd do it, didn't dare to go against him, and maybe, if Daddy went to the pub, Roland could have a shower in peace, alone, without him for company, watching while sitting on the closed toilet lid.

But that was a lie he told himself. Something else always happened after he'd mowed the grass.

He dressed under Daddy's watchful eye, then followed him downstairs. Daddy had brought some mince home and was going to make a cottage pie. He said salads were for wimps, so they'd have hearty food instead. It'd be too heavy, too stodgy for a summer day, but it was better than going hungry.

Roland went into the back garden to the shed and turned the key in the padlock. He swung the door wide and surveyed the jumbled mess inside, so many things stored there, propped up, balancing, wedged into small places. The edges were crammed with stuff on floor-to-ceiling wooden shelves, and the middle was waist high with packing boxes, his old bike with stabilisers in there somewhere, an abundance of junk. On top of it all was the lawn mower, lurching drunkenly, and he dragged it off, thumping it onto the grass.

Daddy eyed him from the kitchen window.

Roland picked up the extension lead from beside the door and carried it in the house, conscious of being monitored.

"I want stripes," Daddy said.

Roland could never make stripes, not with the electric mower, and he thought he was told to do it so the Punishment seemed justified afterwards. He sighed and plugged the extension in, then unravelled it from its plastic casing, which spun with each pull. Daddy liked it put away neatly, the cord tight in rows, and woe betide him if he didn't do that. When he was bigger, he'd wrap it round however the hell he liked, all messy, even with a dangling figure of eight just to be extra rebellious.

He pushed the mower plug into the extension and trudged up and down the garden with the mower, trying desperately to create stripes. Once again, they weren't happening, and he knew exactly what that meant. On the last section, his legs went to jelly, and he struggled to complete it, sickened by fear.

He hated the Punishment.

Daddy still stood by the window, staring out, and he shook his head as if disappointed, then smiled, a big horrible one that churned Roland's stomach. Knots formed in there, squeezing, tightening. Sweat coated his face, and not just from the sun either.

He switched the mower off and put it away, wishing he could lock himself in the shed so Daddy wouldn't take him to that place. *But there was nothing to attach the padlock to inside, and Daddy could easily break the door down.*

He'd just have to grin and bear it.

Or cry and not bear it.

He took his time, but it was just to delay the inevitable. He went into the house, and Daddy frowned at him, standing so tall Roland had to crane his neck.

"Down to the shop with you then," he said.

Roland walked out the front to the car. Daddy drove them two streets away to his butcher's shop, and while he fiddled with deactivating the alarm, Roland tried not to pee himself. He'd been brought here as far back as he could remember, to learn to do as he was told, and while he didn't mind the actual shop, it was a certain room that brought the nightmares.

Inside, Daddy pushed Roland on his back, urging him towards it. There was a special handle that locked you in if you were inside, and no matter how many times he'd tried to get free, he hadn't so far.

Daddy pulled the handle.

A gust of raw meat and fat wafted at him, and that smell, in the shop, was fine, but here, when it came out in an invisible cloud of ice . . .

"Get in."

Daddy shoved him again, and Roland stumbled forward, heading for a cow hanging directly in front of him. He smacked into it, and the rind was so cold and clammy on his cheek. He'd learnt not to put his hands out, because if they touched it, they'd be greasy the whole time he was in there, adding to his torment.

"Half an hour," Daddy said. "Go and put the little light on."

The door snapped shut, and Roland hopped away from the cow. He hadn't counted how many other animals there were, and where they hung — Daddy's shove had caught him off guard — so his walk through to the back of the room would be a minefield. He could bump into them at any moment.

The chilly air hurt his chest, as it always did. Arms out in front, hands curled into fists — better to have the dampness of rind on his outer skin than on his palms — he moved one step to the side, gauging he was in the gap between cows. He shuffled forward, conscious that Daddy would expect the light to come on quickly, which put more pressure on Roland and his bladder. If he wet himself in here, he'd be in so much trouble, so he held it in and walked on.

The hairs on his fingers rose, and he sensed an animal. He stepped left, continued, and in the end, it all got too much, the guessing. He charged ahead, smacking into carcases every which way he turned, and now he didn't know where the back of the room was. He was at a wall, so he pressed his palms to it and felt along as he walked, out of breath, his chest so tense.

No light switch on this one.

He carried on to the next and, at last, his fingers brushed it. He pressed, and the room lit up. A cow was right there, in the corner with him, and he screamed, even though he'd known the bodies were there. But they were so pale, so hairless, and nothing like they were in the fields, and the pigs, they had trotters — Daddy sold them to the old man who came in, every single one of them.

Why did he want so many? What did he do with them?

Roland's nightmares said he kept little boys and girls in his cellar and choked them with the trotters by pushing them down their throats, and when the man came into the shop, Roland always ran out the back.

Heart thrumming, he concentrated on breathing shallowly, waiting, waiting for what was to come.

The voice startled him coming from a hidden speaker, as it generally did, and he imagined Daddy waited so long to speak so Roland relaxed, thinking he wasn't going to do that today.

"Move to cow three," Daddy said.

The hooks were in rows on poles at the ceiling, then there was a chain and another hook attached to the animals, which hung in random spots. Roland rushed between them all to the front of the room and had to work out which one was number three. Yes, there were three in the first row, but was Daddy going from the left today or the right? What had he done last time?

The left had been number one. Three had been on the far right.

"Left," Roland said, going for the opposite.

"Wrong. Three is left, yes, but front left is number one, then number two behind it, and then three after that."

Roland stared at the first line on the left. Daddy had never switched it up like this before. Cruel laughter bellowed, and Roland bit back a whimper.

"Move to number three."

Roland did that and stood by a cow that was so huge he felt tiny.

"Lick its back."

Roland swallowed, tears burning, and closed his eyes. Inched his head forward until his tongue tip touched the animal.

"Not like that, flatten your tongue."

He obeyed, and the taste . . . he'd never get used to it.

"Now go to the other side and get inside the body cavity."

Oh God, oh God . . .

His knees knocked, and his stomach hurt so much. He'd have to touch it, get mess on his hands . . . But Daddy had been kind for some reason, and instead of Roland having to work with all his might to pull the ribs to create a space big enough for him, half of the ribs were gone, cut away with the saw — he knew it was the saw from the marks left behind.

"Don't close your eyes."

Roland pushed his whole body inside and stared ahead at the red meat behind a creamy film of membrane. The stench was so strong.

"Sniff."

Roland inhaled and gagged.

"Fresh . . . is . . . best," Daddy said in a scary voice that was deeper than usual, and he paused between words as if out of breath, and he sounded just like he did when he licked Roland and he — "Oh yes, sniff . . . and . . . lick. Do it, boy."

Roland had no choice but to follow Daddy's orders. He licked the membrane, sniffed it loudly so hopefully the microphone in this terrifying room picked it up.

"You're not doing it enough. Make the cow sway."

Roland went faster, licking and sniffing alternately, and Daddy's breathing stuttered out of the speakers. In an act of defiance, Roland snapped his eyes shut and pretended he licked ice cream, and it was strawberry with chopped peanuts and red syrup.

"Stop. Get out."

Daddy meant out of the cow, not the room, he always did, so Roland opened his eyes and jerked free. Gone was the sweet imaginary taste of strawberries, replaced with the truth — animal, a hint of blood. A lump of fat had attached to his fringe, tick-tocking from side to side. Roland heaved. When he was a man, he'd shave his hair off so this would never happen again when he put his head inside cows.

"Now search for the order."

Roland walked between them all, checking their outer parts for the message written with marker pen. He couldn't find it, and panic welled up, then there it was, right there on a pig, written around its snout.

LICK MY NOSE.

Hot tears scalded his cheeks. The nose had hairs growing out of it, and they looked bristly and hard. Roland took a deep breath and did what Daddy had said, his tongue sliding up a nostril at one point. Bile rose, burning the back of his throat, and he swallowed it down.

"Time's up."

The half an hour had gone quickly today, and he wondered how long he'd been inside the cow. He staggered to the door and waited for the count of sixty-three seconds, then it opened, and Daddy stood there, his cheeks flushed.

"While you cut the grass, I didn't watch you all the time," he said. "I mashed the potatoes and cooked the mince for the cottage pie, and there's something in it you need. Look at you, crying and snivelling. You're a wimp."

Roland swiped the tears away, and the movement dislodged the piece of fat on his fringe. It fell off and landed on the floor with a soft thwap*.*

"Do you want to know what I put in it?" Daddy asked.

Roland nodded. He didn't want to know, God, he didn't, but Daddy would tell him anyway.

"Testicles. I'll make a man of you yet."

* * *

The cow — Angela — swung on her hook just like those others had back in his youth, except it wasn't cold in the back of the artic, not with his halogen heater on, plugged in to his little generator. She was in the way, trying to get close to him while he hung Julieanne Lynch next to her. Why did they always do that, get funny when an extra mummy arrived? Jen was in a grump, too, her sticker smile on the floor again, as well as the knives.

They all became cows once a new one took their place.

He stood and waited for them to stop wavering, and once they'd all stilled, he climbed two steps of the ladder and hugged Julieanne around her waist, her belly to his cheek. He sniffed her body-from-the-coffin scent, so needed, so wonderful, then let her go, giving her a shove. She bashed into Angela, and Angela jostled Jen, then Jen tapped the next one in the row, a ripple of dead bodies, all the mummies dancing. For him. Giving him their time. Making up for the days, the months, and the long years when they hadn't.

Bitches, the lot of them.

Stop that. They're not bitches. Remember the Enlightenment.

Remember the things that ground you. The hook. The smell. The feel. Revolting. Beautiful. Safe.

Roland steadied Julieanne and climbed one step higher. He leant close, closer still, his nose pressed to her cheek, and breathed in the scent of her pallid skin, the faint aroma of make-up the funeral director had put on, something to get her all pretty for viewings. He licked her while all the others moved on their hooks, some spinning from the force of the domino effect. And he remembered that time in the meat room, being inside the cow, and asked himself, "What would it be like to be inside *you*, Mummy?"

He got down, rushed over to his kitchenette, and stroked the cleaver in the drawer, one from Daddy's shop. He could cut her, slice her right down the middle, and her innards, they'd spew out, slapping on the floor. He'd remove everything inside her, scooping it, tearing it with his bare hands, stuff getting under his nails, and he'd bite it all out, swallow it. Taste it, love it.

And there he knelt, over Julieanne, who was prone on the floor, and he'd done all those things, using whatever the hell had been close enough to clip her ribs and throw them to the side, her cavity wide open, and he'd thought he'd been standing at the drawer, when he hadn't, he fucking well hadn't.

"Oh yes, sniff . . . and . . . lick. Do it, boy."

Roland tipped forward, his head landing inside her, flesh against his face.

She smelt beautiful.

He sniffed. He licked. And did that funny breathing Daddy had done until wet heat filled his pants and he shuddered.

He loved Mummy, inside and out.

CHAPTER ELEVEN

Owen got up at the arse crack of dawn, excited at the prospect of working for Len. He'd chatted to him on occasion in the Crow, and he was just as nice as Dave. That was the only downside to this. Dave being dead was why Owen was having to start again elsewhere, and although he'd contemplated leaving, going to college and whatever, and had grumbled to himself about the job and the customers, he hadn't meant it, not really. Maybe some of Dave's customers would go to the butcher in the shopping centre now, and Owen wouldn't have to put up with them. It'd be nice if he didn't have to serve Katherine Willows and hear her barking dog, and then there was Marlene and her lies about Spanish men — *and* her bloody purse she'd got for a bargain. Who cared?

He drove round the back of the shops, almost going past Len's and down to Dave's. Force of habit. An unexpected lump filled his throat, and he swallowed, fighting back tears. Maybe the shock was just setting in, him realising properly that Dave was dead, never coming back, and his shop would close. Dave had told him his ex-wife would sell it if anything happened to him.

What a shame Owen didn't have the money to buy it off her.

He parked in Len's yard, and apprehension eclipsed the wave of sadness. It was time to do what that copper, Wilkins, had said. Take the job. Owen still had some living to do, and Dave being in pieces on a slab didn't mean Owen could take his foot off the accelerator.

I'm doing this for Mum, to help her pay the bills.

He got out of the car and knocked on the back door. The blind was down, same as the one on the window, and he had to admit, he was earlier than Len had said. Maybe he should wait until bang on eight, then knock again. Len might not even be in yet. A car not being in the yard didn't mean anything. Len's wife always collected him out the front in the evenings. Owen had seen her waiting at the kerb.

He shrugged and turned the handle. Sod it, he'd go inside, offer to make Len a cuppa, get in there with a good first impression. He stepped straight into an office, which threw him a bit because he was used to Dave's layout.

But this isn't Dave's; nothing's the same anymore. Get over it.

If the place was unlocked, Len must be here. The morning was another gloomy one, so it stood to reason the desk light would be on. All right, nothing to see. Nothing to get alarmed about.

He walked through into the cutting room, and it smelt of the same cleaner he used at Dave's, some powder that you mixed with water, stuff that was okay around food. But the hose . . . Oh God, the hose was a mess, and it had twisted up into an eight, just like last time.

He staggered into the wall, pain flouncing through his shoulder at the impact, heart thundering, his pulse thudding too fast. He pushed off, away from it, because if this was another crime scene . . .

Don't be daft. It can't happen twice.

"Hello?" he called.

A clock ticked somewhere.

A tap dripped.

He wandered around, poking his head into the meat room, also in the WC, then he moved into the shop. It was fine, nothing out of place, and the empty till drawer stuck out, so this was nothing like when he'd gone to Dave's shop for his phone. Len had removed the takings, probably stored them in the safe.

He went to the front and reached out to pull the blind back but stopped. On the white stripes . . . Faint blood? He retreated, then spun and legged it to his car. There was a flat upstairs, but someone else lived there and accessed it from the front. He drove around there and left the car outside Stobbart's, hammering on the flat door.

A loud scrape and rumble, then someone poked their head out of the window. A bloke, brown hair tousled. "What d'you fucking want at this time of the morning?"

"Um, did you hear anything in the shop below?"

"When?"

"I don't know. Last night? *In* the night?"

"You've got to be bloody joking. No, I was at my old dear's place for her birthday. Got back about two. Crashed." He dipped his head back in and slammed the window down, another scrape and rumble.

"Shit!" Owen patted his coat pocket where he'd put that detective's card, fishing it out. He slumped in the driver's seat and jabbed in her number, his fingers seeming thick, and he pressed a wrong digit. "Fucking hell!" He started again, and then it rang, and relief swamped him for a moment.

"DI Bethany Smith," she said.

"It's me, Owen. Owen Givens."

"How can I help you?"

"I think it's happened again. At Len Stobbart's."

"What?"

"He . . . he's not here. I came, like he told me to, but the back of the shop was open, the yard entrance, and I'm sure there's blood on the front blind."

"Where are you?"

"In the high street. I came round here in my car to speak to the tenant in the flat."

"Stay where you are. We'll be right there."

She was definitely going to think it was him now. He hadn't met Charlotte last night, and his mum had been at bingo. There was no one to vouch for him.

Shit.

CHAPTER TWELVE

Bethany and Mike had suited up and done a check of Stobbart's, and she'd given Isabelle a ring afterwards. SOCO were needed. The back door must have been jimmied, and a message was written on one of the animals in the meat fridge: CAN YOU CREATE STRIPES? A red marker had been stuffed up a pig's hairy nose, and that wasn't something she imagined a butcher would do to his stock. The hose was a mess, like at Dave's, the same figure of eight created.

Bethany had no bloody idea what any of that meant, but it would be something to do with Grey Puffa, and once she found the little bastard, she could ask him what it was. Whether he told her was a different matter. Some of them liked to keep secrets.

They'd also found a pair of yellow headphones sticking out from beneath the front of the glass counter, so either a customer had dropped them, or the killer had, or they'd belonged to Len. DNA from them would sort that puzzle out.

Outside, while they waited for the van, she'd spoken to the man in the flat above. He'd hung out of the window, pissed off at being disturbed, seeing as "That stupid dick-head's woken me up once already!" She'd introduced herself, and he'd soon changed his attitude. Her asking him for an alibi had sent him pale.

Fran was currently looking into his story of being at his mother's until he'd arrived home about two a.m. Leona was on CCTV of the high street, not only searching for the tenant but Puffa as well. She'd confirmed that no camera had caught a vehicle near Wallflower Cemetery. Tammy had taken over CCTV of the outbound roads with the help of uniforms, searching for the car that had left the street behind the shops yesterday, carrying Dave's body, plus for the same vehicle leaving in the past few hours, undoubtedly with Len Stobbart inside it.

Poor Owen Givens shook from head to foot, and he stepped back as a SOCO van coasted up to the kerb.

"Go home, love," Bethany said.

He got in his car and drove away, and she dreaded to think what he'd feel like for the rest of the day. As if discovering one empty shop wasn't bad enough. While he'd said he didn't have anyone to verify his alibi, she'd assured him uniforms would be sent to question his neighbours. Someone may have seen him, especially as he hadn't closed the curtains while he'd watched TV, like he'd said.

Isabelle jumped out of the van and came around the back to swing the doors open. SOCOs joined her, and everyone put protectives on. The wind made for a fight with the paper boiler suits, which flapped every way imaginable.

In full gear, Isabelle came up to Bethany. "Morning. Same as at Dave's?"

"There's another message on an animal, and a marker pen up a pig's nose. The hose is the same mess as before. As far as I can see, all implements are on a rack above the cutting table, but without asking someone who knows how many are meant to be there, some could be missing. I didn't spot any blood in there, but it could be too small to notice. I did, however, see some on the blind over the front door. Looks like the killer's tried to clean it off. If it isn't human, I assume it's from an animal and possibly old."

"Right." Isabelle sighed. "Have you checked your emails? Presley sent us something."

"I haven't had the chance. Owen Givens rang me just as I picked Mike up for work. We came straight here."

"Well, it's to say Dave was strangled. Post-mortem bruises came out on the neck. A man's hands, going by the size of the imprints, fingers close together, more pressure/deeper bruising where the thumbs rested below the Adam's apple, and he's suggesting Dave was raised while being throttled."

"What, so Dave stood on a chair or something?"

"No, more like the killer grabbed his neck and lifted him off his feet to kill him."

Mike tutted. "Christ. You've got to have some strength in your arms to hold a bloke up for an extended amount of time. What's that, three to five minutes to kill that way?"

"Unless he blacked out quickly and the murderer lowered him to finish him off," Isabelle suggested. "Either way, the bruises tell the story."

"Still, that's immense upper core strength as well," Mike mused. "So, are we looking at someone who works out?"

"I just thought the same thing." Bethany took her gloves off. "We should go down to the gym and see if they recognise Puffa Man." She explained to Isabelle about Owen drawing the picture. "You don't know him by any chance, do you?" She took her phone out and showed her the image.

"Eww, that's an unfortunate face." Isabelle shuddered. "He looks exactly what you expect a killer to be — weird and frightening. Dead eyes or what. No emotion in them. And no, never seen him before. Me and Aradul tend to go to pubs where we won't bump into any of you lot."

"So glad that's working out." Bethany smiled.

"What better boyfriend than a forensic tech? We can chat shit about work and not bore the other half." Isabelle popped her face mask over her mouth. "Anyway, I need to get on. By the way, if you didn't gather, even with Presley's email, he's got Dave now. Angela's coffin has been taken in, as has a load of mud, and both are being tested. Might be a few days before we get a hit from the mud, if anything. One of my teams is still out there finishing off. Oh, and the casts created from the footprints . . . Size ten, and the footwear is a boot, although we're still narrowing down the make because some of the treads are so similar they could be mistaken for being the same brand. I'll send you details once I have them."

"Thanks."

"And I have someone going through the crime scene photos under magnifiers before we do in the hope they spot something the naked eye missed." Isabelle shrugged. "Not that us three will be able to get to them soon, because of this." She pointed at Stobbart's. "Someone who has a beef with butchers. Did you like what I did there?"

Bethany groaned. "Christ, woman. Don't pack in your day job. I'll see you later. Unfortunately, we need to go and see Len Stobbart's wife. She hasn't rung in to say he's missing, and I want to know why."

Bethany drove down the high street and parked outside the gym. They entered the reception, which smelt of sweat and deodorant. She approached a muscled blond fella who stood talking to a slender woman in yoga gear. He looked across at them, and the woman disappeared around the corner, her black ponytail swishing.

"Wanting ta join up?" he asked, his Irish accent thick, and he rubbed his hands as if imagining their subscriptions landing with a loud *kerching* in his bank account.

"Um, no time for the gym," Bethany said. *Not to mention the energy*. She showed her ID. "Are you the owner?"

"Aye."

"We're here to ask if you've seen this man." She took her phone out.

"Bloody hell, I thought you were going to say someone else has been murdered. We had coppers in here yesterday about Dave over the road, so we did. Nice bloke. Always gave me cheap steaks."

Bethany held out her mobile, and he leant over to peer at the image.

"No, he's not a member here, and I'd remember him if he was. I tek photos for customer ID cards, see, and there's no way I'd forget that bloke."

Shit. "Okay, what about your employees?"

He popped his head around the corner. "Karen, can ye come here a sec, please?"

The yoga woman appeared, smiling. "Yes?"

"Look at that fella there, will ye?" He jerked a thumb.

Bethany lifted her phone. "Seen him?"

"God, he's the weirdo with the rubber testicles," Yoga said, tweezered eyebrows going high.

"Ye what?" The gym owner gaped. "Been that close to him, have ye?"

Yoga frowned. "What do you mean?"

"Ye know, close enough to find out he's got rubber balls. And who has them anyway? Is it something ye get off the NHS if ye lose your own?"

"No!" Yoga swatted his arm. "He's the gimp from the shopping centre. Sandra told me about him."

The balloon lady. "Are you friends with her?"

"Not as such," Yoga said, "but everyone knows Sandra. She sells cards and balloons in the shopping precinct. She mentioned a bloke sniffing rubber testicles. She actually took a photo of him with her phone and showed me when I went to her stall. I needed a card for my mum's birthday."

"Thanks for your help." Bethany legged it outside with Mike, and she led the way to the precinct.

While the main doors were open, none of the shops were as it wasn't quite nine o'clock yet, but a stall stood outside Volton's, bedecked with helium balloons that bobbed and swayed as a woman tied more on. Lots of *Frozen* and *PJ Masks*, and a shiny silver elephant with a curved sink-drain trunk.

"She's not ill today then," she said to Mike and made a beeline for her. "Excuse me. Sandra, is it?"

The lady, around forty or so, nodded, her over-processed blonde hair shivering, the ends cotton-woolly. She finished securing a balloon to a plastic ring on the side of the stall and straightened. "Yes . . ."

"DI Bethany Smith and DS Mike Wilkins." She let her check her ID. "We understand you have a picture of a man that you took. He was asked to leave the premises after swearing and playing with some rubber balls."

"Oh, him. A right weirdo if ever there was one." She dipped her hand in her waist apron pocket, the sort used to put money in, and produced a phone. Scrolling, she said, "He's not been in since, not that I've seen anyway, but he freaked me out, I have to say. Here he is, look."

Bethany stared down at him. He was partially turned away, but it was clear Owen had drawn him correctly. There was no doubt in Bethany's mind that this was the same man — *and* he had sore skin around his mouth. "Can you send that to me, please?" She handed over her card so Sandra had her mobile number.

"Of course. What's he done? I *knew* he was a nutter." She went on to repeat the story Noel and the CCTV men had given. "So you can imagine why I was unsettled. Who sniffs those? And where did he even get them?"

That's a thought. I'll ask the team to find out online. "I can't see from this picture, but what exactly were the balls like?" What a thing to be asking. Never in her lifetime had she expected to discuss the appearance of rubber testicles with a member of the public. Funny where paths took you.

"Oh, you know, same as the real thing, just rubber. Light pink. Two sacs, wrinkles on them and everything. Very lifelike." Sandra blushed and pressed SEND. "That should be with you now."

Bethany's phone bleeped, and she checked to make sure it had come through. "Yep, that's great. So had you seen him here before that day?"

"No. I wouldn't have taken any notice of him if it wasn't for the swearing. Like I said just now, I had kiddies here to buy balloons while he was wittering on, and I caught the word 'bitch' and looked over. Then he said something about his mum being one, except she wasn't, and it was as though he was arguing with himself. He just came off as unstable, know what I mean? Like he was antsy, upset about something."

"Do you know if he went into the butcher's before he sat on that bench?" Bethany pointed to it.

"I don't know. I had an old lady here asking about birthday cards, then she kept me talking. She left, then the kids came, and I noticed him."

"Do you know the old lady's name?" She was asking for a miracle.

"No, sorry."

"Okay, thanks very much for this. Massive help." She took Sandra's full name, address, and phone number, said goodbye, and walked out alongside Mike. In the fresh air, the wind still gusty, she turned to him. "Who the fuck *is* he?"

"No idea."

She sent the photo to Fran: GET THE PIC OUT TO UNIFORMS. I WANT THEM ON THE LOOKOUT FOR HIM. SOMEONE NEEDS TO BE ONLINE CHECKING WHERE YOU CAN BUY RUBBER TESTICLES.

> Fran: ERR, OKAY, I WON'T ASK . . . UPDATE: THE TENANT ABOVE STOBBART'S IS IN THE CLEAR. NUMEROUS PEOPLE AT HIS MOTHER'S PARTY SAW HIM THERE, CONFIRMING HIS ARRIVAL AND EXIT TIMES, AND CCTV PUTS HIM ENTERING HIS FLAT IN THE HIGH STREET AT SEVEN MINUTES PAST TWO IN THE MORNING. THERE'S NO OTHER ENTRANCE, AND HE DIDN'T LEAVE AGAIN, ONLY APPEARING AT THE WINDOW WHEN HE SPOKE TO OWEN EARLIER. NO ONE ELSE WAS NEAR STOBBART'S ONCE HIS LAST CUSTOMER LEFT, AND ONLY THE BIN MEN APPEARED

AT FIVE-FIFTEEN BEFORE OWEN TURNED UP.

Bethany: THANKS.

She read Fran's message to Mike. "So he entered via the back, like at Dave's."

"Makes sense. Why change what worked before?" he said. "Besides, with CCTV, he'd be thick if he used the front. Which reminds me. Any news on where he parked in the market square yesterday?"

"I'll ask Leona." She messaged her while they walked to the car and got in.

Leona: STILL TRYING TO WORK OUT THE MAKE OF THE CAR FROM THE ROOF, BUT DURING THE TIME HE'D HAVE PARKED, EIGHTEEN VEHICLES WERE SPOTTED ON THE ROAD THAT LEADS TO THE CAR PARK. NO NUMBER PLATES VISIBLE, AS THE CAMERA IS TOO HIGH UP AND IS CONCENTRATED MORE ON THE JEWELLER'S PLACE — REMEMBER THE THEFTS RECENTLY? SO AGAIN, ALL WE HAVE TO GO ON IS ROOFS. IT'S GOING TO TAKE A WHILE.

Bethany: THANK YOU.

"Fuck it," she said and explained what was going on. "Nothing is ever straightforward. I'm gathering there are no other cameras in that area, besides the one for the car park, which didn't help us at all anyway. Roofs. Lots of them. No clear idea of what colour because CCTV is monochrome. How bloody brilliant." She poked Stobbart's home address into the satnav then peeled away from the kerb.

"We'll find him eventually, you know we will."

"Eventually isn't good enough, though, is it." She sighed, annoyed with herself. "Soz for snapping, but sodding hell, I get so frustrated. I swear, if I hadn't made a promise to Vinny after he died to keep going at work, sometimes I'd walk away, do something else."

"But if you walk away, you'll think about him all the time. Then what'll happen?"

She'd crumble. "Hmm. Just put this down to a shitty day then."

"That's the spirit. The weather doesn't help. When it's crap like this, I don't exactly feel chipper. It affects the mood something chronic."

"Definitely. God, here we are. Just what we need, passing on the worst news first thing of a morning." She drove up Stobbart's driveway and cut the engine beside a white Vectra. At the front door, she waited for Mike to join her. Hand raised to knock, she was startled when the door swung inwards. "Mrs Stobbart? Emily?"

"Yes?" The woman's blonde bob reached her jawline, a blunt cut. Her blue eyes filled with tears, the end of her nose pink. "Sorry, I haven't got time if you're selling or canvassing. I was just about to go out."

Bethany produced her ID. "DI Bethany Smith. This is DS Mike Wilkins. We need to come in."

Emily's hand flew up to flutter around her neck. Bethany hid a shudder. If her husband had been killed the same way as Dave, Emily's action seemed macabre.

"What . . . Why?" Emily blinked, and the tears spilt.

"It's regarding Len." Bethany grasped the woman's elbow. "Come on, let's go inside."

She ushered her into the living room while Mike closed the front door. With Emily seated on the sofa looking up at her, Bethany had sympathy. She smiled and sat beside her.

"Did Len come home last night?" Bethany asked.

Emily shook her head. "No. Or I assume he didn't. He wasn't in bed when I woke up this morning, and I phoned the shop — he owns Stobbart's in the high street — but there's no answer. He stays once a week to do the books, so I didn't worry when he wasn't back by bedtime because he gets a taxi on those nights to save me picking him up so late. I went up as usual about ten. What's happened? I heard about Dave, and my mind has gone *there* now you're here."

"Do you know this man?" Bethany showed her the image from Sandra.

Emily nodded. "Oh God. I'll never forget him. He was in the shop the other day. I always pick Len up, you see, and that man was holding him up from closing. I went in to chivvy them along, and he, that man, stared at me so hard I shook. He's got a piercing glare, the kind where you feel you're being assessed and you know he doesn't like what he's seeing."

Bethany understood that. In her experience, some men undressed you with their eyes or probed deep somehow, leaving you feeling dirty and uncomfortable. "I see. Did he speak to you?"

"Well, he stomped out when I said 'chop-chop!' and muttered 'bitch' as he went past. Len couldn't have heard, because if he had, he'd have gone out there and had a go at him, telling him he wasn't welcome anymore. I kept it to myself. Even if I'd told Len afterwards on the way home, he'd have said something to him the next time he came in. Len's soft-hearted, but when it comes to me or the kids, the gloves are off."

Bitch. Same as he'd said by Sandra's balloon stand. "We've got some unsettling news, Emily. We believe this man killed Dave. This morning, we were called out to your husband's shop by Owen Givens, who was supposed to start work for Len today."

"Supposed? What do you mean? There's no supposed about it. Len told me Owen was with us now that Dave can't employ him."

"Owen can't work because he found the doors unlocked and the shop empty."

Emily wailed, and it was obvious she'd caught on to the implications of that. Bethany whispered for Mike to ask Rob on the front desk to get uniforms out to Wallflower and Dullbourne to check for new grave disturbances, plus ring Alice Jacobs, the FLO, and he left the room, closing the door to. Emily cried for a while, gripping Bethany's hand. Once she'd calmed a little, Bethany deemed it appropriate to continue. Suspected murder or not, she had to plug on regardless of Emily's feelings.

"It may not be the same scenario as Dave's," she said, softening it a bit, "but you understand we have to act as though it is. With Len not being in the shop, we've come to the conclusion that you probably have. Now, while it may not be the case here, I'm going to be investigating that line of enquiry anyway, all right?"

Emily nodded, staring into space. "I told him to do the books at home last night, what with Dave . . . I said it might not be safe."

"Why didn't he do that?"

"I'm not sure. He has a habit of brushing off my concerns."

"We visited Len yesterday to warn him to be vigilant, to be careful, and I'd say he took that advice on board because the back door had been broken into, so he *had* locked up. Why butchers are being targeted, we don't know, but I'll try my level best to find out." She winced at the thought of her next question. "Forgive me for this, but you said you went to bed about ten. Can anyone confirm that?"

Emily snapped out of her stare and looked at Bethany. "You think it's me?" It came out as a squeak.

"No, I don't, honestly, but I have to ask these things."

"No one was here. I watched two episodes of *Deadwater Fell* on catch-up because I'd forgotten to put them on every week, and then it was bed."

"Thank you. Now, Mike's getting our family liaison officer here for you, okay? You can also have your children here, of course, and—"

"The children . . ." That set her off again, and she hung her head, which bobbed with every sob.

Mike came back in and nodded, mouthing, "Five minutes." Then, "I'll make you a cuppa, Emily." He walked out again.

"Would you like me to contact your children?" Bethany asked.

"They'll be at work by now. Oh God, how do I tell them something like this?"

"Just send them a text and ask them to come round, stressing it's important. That way, they won't be worrying to such a degree that they drive erratically. The last thing you need is accidents on top of this."

Emily got up and took her phone off the TV cabinet. She sat and handed it to Bethany. "We have a group chat on Messenger. You do it. Pretend to be me."

Bethany accessed the home screen — no PIN — then selected the correct app. She fired off a message and waited for responses: *What's wrong? Are you okay?* Bethany typed again. *Just come here.* She placed the phone on the sofa.

"They'll know it's bad for me to ask them here like that." Emily sniffed and cuffed her nose with her cardigan sleeve.

Mike came in and handed her some strong tea.

She took it with a shaking hand. "How did Dave die?"

Bethany didn't know whether to answer that or not. She glanced at Mike, who shook his head: *She's not ready for that yet.*

"We're not sure at present." Bethany hated herself for lying.

The doorbell pealed a melody, and Mike went off to answer it. Alice came in with him and introduced herself, getting straight down to it with her calming influence. Mike would have told her what was going on when he'd phoned her.

"We'll be leaving now, Emily." Bethany stood and glanced out of the window. "A red car has just pulled up. One of your kids?"

"That'll be my son."

Alice had to take the tea away as Emily flopped back onto the sofa to cry.

Bethany left the house, a man streaking past her up the path and stopping Mike to ask what was happening.

In the car, she took a moment to have an emotional breather, alone, and her phone rang, fate having other ideas. She closed her eyes for a second then answered it. "Hi, Rob."

"Dullbourne Cemetery. Black bags at a Julieanne Lynch's grave."

"Fuck it. Just fuck it." She sighed out a long breath. "Sorry. It's been a traumatic morning already."

"I can imagine. I've let Isabelle know, and she said she'd meet you there. Fair warning, she had a bit of a grumble because all three of her teams are out now, one still at Dave's, another at Stobbart's, the third at Wallflower, and now she has to pinch a couple of people from each one to go with her to Dullbourne."

"Cheers for that. We'll go there now. Bye." She tapped out a message to Fran to let her know one of them needed to come to Emily's to question her children regarding their whereabouts last evening and overnight, asking her to give them an hour to let the news sink in about their father. She requested that Leona look at CCTV around Dullbourne to see if they could catch Puffa — or anyone else — in a vehicle there.

Mike plopped into the passenger seat, his features twisted. "I absolutely hate bolshy twats."

"Son give you trouble, did he?"

"Yep. Let's go before the daughter arrives. If she's anything like him . . ." He jabbed his seat belt in to lock it.

"Alice will sort them. She's good at that. In the meantime, we're off to Dullbourne Cemetery."

Mike whipped his head round to stare at her. "Tell me you're joking."

"I wish I was, matey, but we have another grave disturbance."

"It never rains but it pours."

"You got that right." She nodded at the windscreen.

The heavens had opened wider, as if crying for Len, each pelt on the glass hard and angry. Thunder growled, dark-grey clouds moved sluggishly, and a streak of lightning ripped into one of them.

"The new crime scene's going to be fucked," Mike grouched.

"Of course it is. A case wouldn't be the same if we didn't have obstacles all the way." She flicked the wipers on and drove off. "Story of our bloody working lives."

CHAPTER THIRTEEN

Years later, and Roland still hated stripes. Daddy had a thing about them, saying the ones on his awning at the shop were proof of his hard work and dedication, that he'd made it, he was somebody of note. He had stripy shirts, stripy ties, stripy bloody trousers. The only thing he couldn't get stripes on was the grass in the back garden. He'd mentioned buying a petrol mower, they were the sort that created lines, but had never purchased one.

Like Roland often thought, that was on purpose. Daddy didn't want him to make them, otherwise, he wouldn't be able to take him to the shop for the Punishment.

Roland sat on the wooden bench out the back of the house, swinging his legs in agitation. Daddy was in the bath and had said for Roland to wait before he cut the grass so he could watch. Roland thought a lot whenever he was alone, asking himself questions he had no answers to.

Why does Daddy like licking me?

Why does he play with my maggot?

Why does it have to grow for him?

He got up, restless, the splashing of water in the bathroom filtering out through the ajar window. He was safe — for now — so walked to the bottom of the garden, thinking about where he was supposed to put the new flowers Daddy had bought. The whole bed near the fence was crammed as it was. He worked out that if he pulled all the ones up that were already there, he could rearrange them and add the rest.

May as well start that now.

He was careful with his little spade, digging around the roots so they didn't get damaged. One by one, he removed the blooms and set them on the grass, some of the mud coming loose and snuggling between the green blades. Daddy would make him use the handheld hoover to suck up all the mess.

It took a good while to tug up every one of them, the noise of splashing water just about reaching him still, so Daddy wasn't out of the bath yet. What did he do in there to make such a racket?

Before him was an expanse of mud with holes it in where the flowers had been. Daddy might be cross if Roland didn't smooth it all over, so he set about doing that, then prepared new holes in regimented lines, like stripes, as per Daddy's instructions. Roland had to dig down a long way for a few of the plants, which had big roots. His spade hit something, and he supposed it was the stones Daddy said were there to help with the drainage. Roland dug on, southwards, needing a well-like space for the small tree he'd yanked out earlier. A cedar, it was, the same sort that was in cemeteries. They had shallow root systems and could be planted anywhere, so Daddy had said.

The next-door neighbour had poked his head over the fence when Daddy had first bought it. "If you plant a cedar in your garden, expect poverty," he'd said. "You should leave it where it is an' all once it's bedded in. Transplanting them — not wise. You do that, then death comes."

"What a load of old shit," Daddy had replied, laughing despite his scowl — he'd been angry but wouldn't show it to anyone except Roland. After all, he had to maintain that he was a nice man, couldn't have anyone thinking otherwise.

The conversation had unsettled Roland, and now he realised what he'd done. He was about to transplant the cedar, so who was going to die? Quickly, he dug even deeper, stabbing at the ground with the tip of his spade, and it hit something hard again. Roland used his hands to shift the mud so he could remove the stone and continue with his job, but it wasn't a stone.

It looked like a bone inside a clear bag.

He scrabbled to push the mud away, revealing more, and there was a skull peering at him from behind a sheet of see-through plastic. He bit his lip to stop a scream coming out. Hair, the same colour as Mummy's, was attached to the top. Shock and horror coursed through him, chased away by happiness and exhilaration that she'd been here, right here *all along, not off with a new boyfriend like Daddy had told him, told everyone. He'd lied, must have hidden her here, because Mummy wouldn't have been able to put herself in that bag and cover her body with mud.*

And here it was, the Enlightenment, the moment he realised, and he used the sharp tip of his spade to break the bag so he could touch her. It did nothing but make a divot, so he ripped it with his hands, and the smell, the smell engulfed him in its disgusting yet wonderful scent, the new aroma of Mummy, nothing like her perfumed self of before.

He sniffed hard and thought of all the nights without her telling him a story. All the days he'd pined for her. All the years he'd waited for her to come back, with Daddy telling him she never would and that it was just him and Roland now, and their maggots, and the licks, and the visits to the meat room at the shop, Roland surrounded by cows, Daddy's way of reminding him that Mummy was one of them, a cow, a bitch, a woman who hadn't loved her son enough to stay.

The gurgle of the water going down the pipe attached to the back of the house meant Daddy was getting out of the bath. Roland's heart-rate picked up speed, and while he wanted to stare at what was left of Mummy, he couldn't. A quick lick of her cheekbone, then he was shoving the cedar in, covering her back up, mud toppling into the hole, around the gnarly roots, hiding her forever. Pain lanced his chest, a really sharp spear, and he wondered if it was from heartache.

Roland let the tears wet his cheeks and worried about the transplantation. Would he die now, like the neighbour had said? He repositioned the flowers, tallest at the back, his mind swirling with the rest of that conversation.

"Cedars contain spirits," the neighbour had informed them. "You plant that there now, and it'll settle, that spirit, and maybe watch over you if you're lucky. But like I say, you dig it up, put it somewhere else later, and the spirit will come for you."

The words had chilled Roland's skin, but Daddy had only laughed.

"Superstitious rubbish," he'd said.

The neighbour had shaken his head. "You'll see. Move it, and your lives will never be the same again."

So what was going to happen? Would the spirit come for Roland because he was the one to move it? Would it murder him?

He nearly wet himself.

"What the bloody hell are you doing?" Daddy shouted.

Roland wiped his cheeks on his T-shirt then looked over his shoulder. "Putting the new flowers in like you said." He'd completed two stripes of them and only had two more to go.

"I didn't ask you to dig them all up, did I?" Daddy stomped across the grass and came to stand beside Roland. He stared at where the cedar was. "Shit. How far down did you go?"

Roland shrugged, wanting to act calm even though he was anything but. Would he have to go to the shop now and lick the cows? "Not far. You told me they didn't have long roots. The trees, I mean."

Daddy sighed out a wobbly breath, and it moved a strand of his damp fringe. "Good. Good."

And Roland knew then, that for a moment Daddy had thought Roland had found Mummy, that he knew where she was and who had put her there. And it had to be Daddy. Roland remembered the bed originally being overturned and new plants being put in, and the cedar, much later, and now, the new flowers, as if Daddy wanted the whole thing covered, disguising her resting place.

Daddy sniffed. "You smell that?"

Roland shook his head. He didn't want to admit it was Mummy, that he'd seen her, smelt her.

"Right then. Get those other flowers in, then do the grass. Oh, and before you do, use the little hoover. You've made a mess. And don't forget, stripes, boy. Stripes."

* * *

Roland hung Julieanne back up and punched the woman in her gaping stomach, annoyed she wasn't Mummy, pissed off she didn't have a plastic sheet over her face, and that she even *had* a face, not a skull. "What do you have to say about that then, eh?"

She didn't answer him.

She was getting on his nerves, dancing like that, even with her belly missing, as if this was a fun time and not one of utter trauma. The memory of the Enlightenment hadn't been as special as it usually was — he hadn't smelt that smell properly, or felt how he'd felt when he'd discovered Mummy down there, or remembered the way the mud had slipped through his fingers, and the taste of her cold bone beneath his tongue when he'd licked her . . . he hadn't gained the same sense of well-being as he had at other times. The remembrance was fading more and more with each recall, and that was why he had to dig these cows up, to reenact it, to get that horror then the high, to have the full brunt of everything hitting him at once, then the fear of Daddy coming, Roland wishing he could chop him up into little bits and stuff *him* in the earth, so he was there instead of Mummy.

"You should be grateful I brought you home," he snarled at Julieanne, "but instead, you're ungrateful by not smelling like all the other mummies."

That bothered him, the lack of a strong stench, and maybe that was because she'd been buried so soon after death, less than a week. Was the embalming fluid masking her true odour, the one that spoke of her lying in a hospital morgue then in a coffin on top of the undertaker's slab fridge for more than a fortnight? He didn't know, *didn't fucking know*, and that was annoying him above all else.

He'd need to find an internet café and look that up: *Why doesn't this dead body smell like the others?*

He gave her another right hook to her side, and it sent her careening into Angela, and once again, Angela whacked Jen, Jen whacked the next one, and on it went until they all danced in mockery, their sticker smiles wide, cruel.

"Fuck all of you bitches."

He put his puffa on — he planned to go out, visit that butcher in the precinct, but instead, he stormed to his bed and flung himself on it, resting on his back and staring at the ceiling, arms dropping by his sides.

Something crackled.

He frowned. Patted his jacket pocket. He pulled out the letter that had been in Julieanne's coffin — he'd forgotten all about it — and now he'd get to see who'd been writing to his mother.

To my dear mum,

Sad that this is the first letter I've ever written to you, and it's the last as well. I wish I'd sent you notes before now, told you exactly how I feel, properly, not just saying 'I love you' in a mad dash for the front door, eager to get on with my own stuff, forgetting, or, if I'm honest, not even thinking about you at home by yourself in the evenings. You've always been so resilient, so self-assured, that it never entered my head you might be lonely without me there, waiting for a snippet of my time and attention, because during the day I'm too busy at work.

I have a taste of that now, the loneliness, what with you being gone, and I can only apologise if I ever made you feel this way. Okay, you've always said I have to live my best life, that you may have given birth to me, brought me up, but it didn't give you the right to any more of my time once I was an adult than I was prepared to give.

I took that literally. I wish I'd ignored your advice, because I have fewer memories, fewer moments to look back on that we shared together. I have a lot, but the years you took care of me will <u>never be enough</u>. Not now you're gone.

Even though you thought I wouldn't, that I wasn't the type, I'd planned to have children, to see your face when your first grandchild was brought to you, and I'd take a picture, preserving it forever. Something to look at, a fond moment, but all I have is a mountain of selfies and other photos with me in them, surrounded by friends. The last one I have of me and you is from eight years ago.

Why didn't I take more of us?

Why did I think you'd be here forever and there was always tomorrow?

Tomorrow is here, without you in it, and I can't even begin to express how sorry I am that I didn't share more of myself with you. There was always something else to do, always somewhere other than home to go, and I breezed about, selfishly, I think, doing whatever I wanted. You'd say it wasn't selfish and it was exactly what I should have been doing, but that would only stand up if you hadn't died, because later, when I'd lived that best life you wanted for me, and I'd calmed down, behaved more maturely, there we'd be, me and you, chatting over a cuppa, laughing, looking forward to the next phase.

There are no more phases with you in them.

I will never forget you. Never forget the lessons you taught me, and every time I see a Red Admiral butterfly, I'll think of that time one flew at your face, and you screamed and ran around the garden like a loon, and I'll laugh through the tears, remembering, recalling, because that's all I have left.

Memories.

So, Mum, here is where I tell you you're the best person I ever knew, the one who selflessly gave up for me, who steered me right. I hear your voice, you know, talking to me in my head, and it's mine really, me pretending you're there, giving me comfort, telling me everything will be okay. But it won't be — how can it? How can things ever be the same again without your laugh, your smile, your everything?

I hurt with the pain of this, wish you were here to cuddle it all away, but you're not, and all I have are my own arms to hug myself with. Another pretence — I close my eyes and tell myself it's you.

We'll meet again one day, and I swear we'll spend all those missed times together, catching up, and it'll be the best, just like you.

Love you, Mum, always.

Yasmin xxx

Rage burbled inside Roland, and hot tears of anger burnt his cheeks. Who the hell did Mummy think she was, having a daughter? And what was this about a best fucking life? She'd wanted this Yasmin bint to be happy, but what about him, her son? Where was *his* best life? *His* memory of the Red Admiral? He was her firstborn, the one she should have been taking care of, but instead, she'd given her all to this little slapper.

He threw the letter on the floor and got up, incandescent, racing towards Julieanne, towards all of them, their swaying reduced to a gentle rock. He punched Julieanne's tits, jealousy rearing its uglier-than-him head, consuming him, goading him to obliterate her, teach her a lesson, one that said: *You don't belong here with me, not now you had her, that Yasmin.*

He reached up and gripped her beneath the armpits and pulled, her scalp ripping off the butcher's hook, and he staggered from her weight, dropping her. He sat on her shins and bent over, stuffing his face inside her cavity, and it wasn't the same as the cow from his childhood. She didn't smell right, didn't have that fine membrane he could lick, so he flattened his tongue and drew it up over the mess in there, and hated her, hated Daddy for still making him want to do this. The meat locker was a cruel, scary place, and what he'd had to do in there even scarier, yet here he was reenacting it.

Most of all, he hated Julieanne for not being Mummy.

He shifted to sit on her pelvis and struck her face, the red mist descending so thick he couldn't see anything. By the time it cleared, Julieanne didn't look like herself anymore, and he got up, weak but intent on finding his sister and giving her the same pasting as he'd given their mother.

But she's not your sister.

Roland stumbled away, stripping his clothes off. "What do you know about my sister?" he asked that voice. "What the fucking hell has any of this got to do with you?"

He showered her stink off him, dressed, and put on a different jacket — the puffa was tainted by Julieanne now. Then he sorted the ramp and drove backwards out of the artic, closed the doors, and headed towards Dullbourne. He'd ask the vicar where Yasmin lived, make out he was a cousin not a brother, and that he needed to find her before he went home to Jamaica Street. Yes, he was going there early, to regroup, to spend some time thinking, because even he could admit his mind wasn't working right.

Yasmin wasn't his sister, he knew that, but the problem was, he didn't care.

CHAPTER FOURTEEN

Len Stobbart had butcher's hooks in his nose. They had been fed up his nostrils. The ends had come through the skin, but there was no blood. Bethany sighed behind her face mask, staring down at the head and the black bag it was in, enclosed by a plastic evidence box. What a fucking mess this case was. While they had a suspect, they had no clue where to find him, which left him free to do this again and again if that was on his agenda.

"We've got to stop this man," she said to Mike. "With Julianne's body missing, we have a serious nutter here."

"Do you think he'll go after Thomas Volton, with the security so high in the precinct?"

"I want to say it's unlikely, but who knows what the back of that shop is like. We need someone to go and have a look at the access point from the rear."

"I'll send Rob a message to get uniform down there."

While he did that, Bethany thought about her team, working like dogs. Fran had taken it upon herself to check the database for other butcher cases, and she'd messaged Bethany the results. While none had died, as far as they knew, ten others in different parts of the country had gone missing, never to be seen again, but only one per location. With many jurisdictions and forces in the UK, it was no wonder two and two hadn't been put together. Unless you were looking for a pattern, the fact that a considerable amount of butchers had disappeared had escaped notice.

The killer had escalated here by offing two. Why?

Bethany had instructed Fran to go and speak to Chief Kribbs, bring him up to date — something Bethany hadn't had time to do yet — and ask him for help in contacting various cemeteries in the vicinity of where the other butchers had lived, working out how many funerals had taken place during those times, and determining which graves could have no bodies in them apart from chopped-up butchers in black bags.

A daunting task, one that meant a lot of officers all over the UK would be in on this case.

This shed new light on things. The killer had to be someone who could travel a lot without it being noticed or seem strange to family members — if he had any. They could be a lone wolf. So was he a salesman? A lorry driver? Haulage companies were being asked if they recognised the man in Sandra's photo, and for their routes so officers could compare them with the locations of the missing butchers. As for the salesman angle, it could be any number of employees in any number of companies.

While enquiries of this ilk would take time, Bethany intended to find him before much manpower had been wasted on chasing up drivers who may have nothing to do with this.

She'd actioned for uniforms to drive round Shadwell and note all lorries parked up in bays or on verges, each driver to be questioned: *Why are you in Shadwell? Who do you work for? What's your current route?* It had to be done, even if nothing came of it. The public outcry if they didn't check and it turned out the killer was parked in plain sight . . . it didn't bear thinking about. Peter Uxbridge, the crime reporter at the *Shadwell Herald*, would have a field day, executing them all with pen to paper. She was surprised the little shit hadn't heard about these deaths yet, seeing as he had someone on the inside in the police force, passing him information.

"All body parts are present," Isabelle said from her crouch in front of the plastic boxes each black bag was in. "Except for the testicles."

Bethany closed her eyes for a moment, then opened them again to glance at Mike. He looked sick to his stomach — probably imagining having his balls lopped off.

"Presley said they were removed from Dave after death," Isabelle went on, "so it's probably the same here with Len. No need to go white as a sheet, Mike."

He shuddered. "I was just imagining the pain, that's all."

"Warped fucker." Isabelle laughed.

"Not like *that*." Mike huffed, indignance written all over him. "I was thinking of how much it may have hurt them."

"Well, the bollocks are the last of our concerns. Going by this," Isabelle gestured to Len's head, "we're looking at another strangulation, but a change in MO as well."

"What do you mean?" Bethany asked.

"He's been stabbed in the stomach and back of the neck by something." Isabelle grimaced. "On the latter, they made the main cut just below the neck — you know, when they sliced his head off — and it seems to me like some sort of filer. Or maybe a chisel."

"I'll be the judge of that." Presley came in.

"That's our cue to go and speak to the vicar." Bethany wanted to be out of the tent if Isabelle started getting lairy with the ME.

Bethany cocked her head at Mike to get him to come with her, then turned to Presley.

"Hello, and goodbye for a bit. Back soon." She left and walked along the cordoned-off path that led to the church, Mike beside her. "What do you make of the stab wound then? Was Len more difficult to strangle, maybe put up a struggle, so he was stabbed to calm him down?"

"Could have used the tool or whatever to break in. We didn't find anything at the scene, so I reckon he had it on him, probably from his car. A tyre iron or whatever." Mike pulled his hood down and lowered his face mask.

Bethany left her hood on but freed her mouth. The wind had a bite to it, but at least the rain had buggered off for now. "Yep. What did you think about us finding those yellow earphones at the shop?"

Mike shrugged. "Who knows. Let's hope the killer dropped them, that's all I can say. At least then we'd have DNA off them, and even if he's not in the database to compare it with, we've got something when we catch him."

"Knowing our luck, they'll be Len's. Actually, to save us wondering, can you give Emily Stobbart a ring and ask her if he owned any?"

"Bloody hell, what if her twatty son answers?"

Bethany got her phone out. "Or how about I do it." She phoned Len's wife, who told her the earphones were her husband's, a recent gift from their daughter. Bethany shoved her phone away, annoyed. "Len's. Typical."

"The killer might have touched them, though. I mean, why were they in the shop anyway? And if that *is* Len's blood on the blind, it means he was possibly killed near there, so maybe he had them on, the killer stabbed him in the neck, and the headphones fell out."

"No idea. And there was a distinct lack of unknown fingerprints at Dave's, they were mainly Dave's and Owen's, so my guess is he used gloves. What killer wouldn't? *Shh* now, we're here." She entered the dusty-smelling church and approached the vicar.

He was around sixty, slim, with thick salt-and-pepper hair, and he dealt Bibles out on pews, probably ready for the next congregation, although she'd already informed him upon their arrival, when he was by the grave, that a service wouldn't be taking place while SOCO were about. Maybe he was doing it to keep his mind occupied.

"We're able to talk to you now," she said. "Sorry about the delay. We had to assess the scene first."

"That's quite all right. It gave me time to reflect alone. For a short while anyway."

What did he mean by that? Was he having a sly dig that they'd interrupted his time by himself? Tough. This was a murder inquiry, not a case of gravestone graffiti or whatever. Him conversing with his inner self or God wasn't top of her priority list.

He dropped the last Bibles in place and sat between two of them, reaching down to fetch a kneeling pad from beneath a pew. He placed it on his belly and hugged it, and she idly thought about the dust from it getting on his clothes.

He cleared his throat. "I had a shock, you know, finding those bags. Absolutely silly of me to have touched the mud and opened one, knowing what was inside them — news travels fast, doesn't it. The groundsman did the same at Wallflower, so I heard."

If he's heard, why is Uxbridge silent and not blabbing about it in the paper?

"He did, yes." She smiled. "While what you did wasn't ideal, don't worry about it now. We have a couple of footprints other than yours there, so that's something. Now, can you take me through what happened?"

She sat three Bibles along to give him some space. Mike stood by the altar, notebook and pen in hand.

"What with all this wind — more like gales — I'd noticed at Julieanne's funeral that one of the tree branches had snapped and was hanging loose. I didn't like to have anyone come out and chop it off while mourners were here so decided to sort it this morning myself. It would also save on church funds if I did it. People can't afford to be so generous these days when putting money in the coffers."

He looked at her as if she ought to be dipping her hand in her pocket.

She smiled sympathetically, working out what cash she had on her. A tenner, most likely, as it was her turn to pay for lunch. "Please go on."

The vicar gave her a disparaging look when she didn't cough up. "I carried the stepladder down there — the tree in question is behind her plot — and I got up to give it a bit of a tug, you know, pull it down." He blinked rapidly. "I yanked a bit too hard and ended up falling off the ladder, right beside the flowers next to her grave. I'm so terribly sorry."

"Again, don't worry. What happened next?"

"I was on my back and glanced over to get my bearings, and there was a mound coming out of the mud. Part of me knew what it was, what with me having heard about the Wallflower incident, and I got up to check. I moved the mud — I'm so ashamed — and opened the bag, and there . . . Oh, dear God, there was a face staring back at me. I knew who he was — it's Len, the butcher, I get my lamb from him — and I staggered back, trampling poor Julieanne's flowers. I made quite a mess of them. So many petals trodden on." He cleared his throat again. "But then I noticed something, and it quite chilled me. Flowers I hadn't stood on were also squashed — they were peeking out through others that were on top. Now, we don't do that, stacking them, we place every bouquet in its own space, so . . ."

"So you think someone else must have moved them, ruined them, and hid them beneath the others?"

He nodded. "Ghastly business. Those flowers are on sacred ground. And while I have no idea whether this is the case here, what kind of person would remove a body and place another there? Surely the same has happened here as it has at Wallflower."

"We have someone in mind. Before I show you who we think it is, have you noticed anyone hanging about lately?"

"Why yes, I have, and he was here again, just a few moments before you walked in."

Bethany's stomach plummeted. More than two minutes must have had passed since they'd entered the church, so he'd be long gone, even on foot, but she glared at Mike to go out there and check anyway. Mike nodded and ran up the aisle.

"What does he look like?" she asked the vicar.

"Let me see. Large nostrils. He's bald, some of the hair growing back. It's black if his eyebrows are any indication. No facial hair other than those. His eyes are wide and round, a bright blue. A wide face, too."

"Where was he when you just saw him?"

"He came in here, asked me if I could tell him where Yasmin Lynch lives. Of course, I said no. You just don't do that, do you, giving out addresses willy-nilly. He said he was her cousin, and I said he'd know where she lived if that were the case, so he went on to say they'd lost contact until the funeral and he'd forgotten to ask her where she lives now."

Why would the killer want anything to do with the daughter?

An uneasy feeling crept into Bethany's stomach, and she excused herself for a moment to send a message. She walked over to the other side of the church.

Bethany: ERICA, CHECK CCTV IN THE VICINITY OF DULLBOURNE FROM UP TO HALF AN HOUR AGO. ROADS LEADING THERE. I WANT ALL CARS CLOCKED.

Then to Fran.

Bethany: FIND OUT WHERE A YASMIN LYNCH LIVES — JULIEANNE'S DAUGHTER — AND SEND UNIFORM ROUND THERE TO MAKE SURE SHE HASN'T GOT A VISITOR, NAMELY, OUR KILLER. ASK THEM TO TAKE THE PHOTO WE HAVE AND ASK HER IF SHE KNOWS HIM.

Fran: DOING IT NOW.

Her phone rang then. Rob. "Yep."

"There's no way anyone can get inside Volton's shop from the back of the precinct. Uniforms have been there, and the door is steel, no handle, just a keyhole."

"Thanks." Bethany returned to the pew. "Sorry about that. So prior to today, when have you seen the man?"

"He's been coming for about a month, walking up and down between graves, as if inspecting them, trying to find the one he wanted. I did ask him a couple of weeks ago what he was doing, and he ran off to a green car."

Bethany's heart somersaulted. "Did you recognise the make?"

"I didn't, sorry, but it was a four-door and resembled a Mini, although it wasn't one of those as I have one myself. At a distance, though, it looks the same. Or maybe that's just me because I only wear my glasses for reading."

"Okay. Two seconds." She sent another message.

> Bethany: FIND OUT WHAT CARS LOOK LIKE MINIS. WE HAVE A GREEN VEHICLE SPOTTED THAT MAY BELONG TO OUR MAN.

To the vicar, "Did you see him any other time?"

"He attended Julieanne's funeral, stood at the back. I thought he'd been here before to see how the graves were tended to, checking if Julieanne was being buried in a decent place. Silly, the things you tell yourself. While the majority of the upkeep here is done by family members, I do a sweep every day to tidy those that haven't had anyone here for a while, and of course, I make sure the gardener comes to cut the grass."

That fucker was at her funeral? "Excuse me again." She stood and walked to the altar this time, phone in hand. She was too antsy to sit still at the minute.

> Bethany: CHECK WHETHER OBITUARIES WENT OUT IN THE LOCAL PAPERS AND ONLINE FOR ANGELA LOCKWOOD AND JULIEANNE LYNCH. THE KILLER NEEDED TO FIND OUT SOMEHOW THAT THE GRAVES WOULD BE NEW. HE WAS

POSSIBLY AT JULIEANNE'S FUNERAL, FOR GOD'S SAKE!

Fran: OKAY. WANT ME TO CHECK ONLINE, FACEBOOK AND THE LIKE, VIA FRIENDS AND FAMILY OF THE DECEASED, WHETHER THEY'VE UPLOADED ANY PICTURES?

Bethany: PLEASE. HE COULD BE IN ONE OF THEM.

She went back to the vicar, getting up the image of the suspect. She sat and showed it to him. "Is this the man you saw?"

He nodded. "Most definitely."

"And you don't know his name?"

"No."

"If he comes back again, you need to let me know." She put her phone away and handed him her card, plus the tenner. "That's for the church. As soon as you see him, tell me. And if he's just looking at graves again, perhaps check the make of his car while he's busy, maybe get the number plate, but only if it's safe to do so."

"Certainly, although I selfishly hope he doesn't come back, for obvious reasons."

She smiled, thanked him, and said goodbye. Out in the stone porch, she waited for Mike, who came towards her out of breath, his hair wet from a soaking. Rain hit him from the side. He'd probably been so intent on catching him he hadn't lifted his hood.

"Have a nice run, did you?" she asked.

"I legged it all around the church, but there's only SOCO here and Nicola stopping people going into the cemetery part. She didn't see anyone leave the church before we entered it — she's round the back so wouldn't have. Basically, he's got away."

She told him what the vicar had said. "So the fucker, pardon me swearing at a church, was actually at Julieanne's funeral. How sick is that?"

Mike shook his head. "Awful."

Her phone bleeped.

Fran: FIAT 500 HATCHBACK, CABRIO. PIC ON THE WAY.

It appeared on her screen, and she nipped back into the church. "Is this the vehicle, sir?"

The vicar looked at it. "I'd say so, yes."

"Thank you."

She rejoined Mike. "Seems this is the car we're after."

Bethany: OKAY, THAT MAY BE THE ONE. DO A SEARCH ON ALL OF THEM. IT'LL HAVE TO BE THE WHOLE BLOODY COUNTRY, WHAT WITH BUTCHER DISAPPEARANCES BEING SO WIDESPREAD. THE ONE WE WANT IS GREEN.

"It'll take hours to sift through all those." She led them back to the tent.

They looked around outside it, and she made a mental note of the broken branch, the fallen-over ladder. The flowers were inside, so they stepped in.

"Those bouquets need bagging as well," she said to Isabelle. "The vicar trod on some, but he said someone else had as well, before he did it."

Isabelle nodded. "Rightio. I spotted some holes beneath these ones, like something had been poked into the earth. I've got hold of my team at Wallflower to see if there are similar there. Could be hooks or something so the killer got down into the hole via ropes."

"More likely a ladder if there are two holes," Mike said. "The width between them is about right."

"I did wonder how he'd got in there," Bethany said.

"The wound to the back of the neck," Presley said, as if their current conversation was of no consequence to him, "was a slightly downwards motion upon entry. I've had a look at the neck, plus the torso where the weapon would have gone in, and it's at an angle consistent with someone making an arc motion from above."

Bethany frowned. "Explain?"

"This fellow here was possibly crouching or kneeling when the killer struck — the entry hole is a square, so a tool of some sort. Strangulation was from behind this time. The fingers were at the front of the neck, the thumbs at the back. The bruising indicates the deceased was slightly lower than the killer, so perhaps his head was on a level with the perpetrator's stomach. I'll know for sure once I study Len better."

"So the headphones could have fallen out if the two men were on the floor tussling," Bethany said.

"Sorry?" Presley appeared confused.

"Just musing to myself. We found over-the-ear headphones, wireless, in the butcher's shop."

"Ah, so that's what it is." Presley reached into the bag that contained the head and turned it over so it was face-down. "See those curved marks behind the ears? Do they resemble the headphones you found?"

Bethany thought about it. "Yes."

"The pressure from being strangled will have meant the skin puffed up, for want of a better description." Presley mimicked having his hands around the neck from behind. The headphones were probably a tight fit as it was, pressing into the skin, so the throttling and the skin pushing against it has made these faint indents, which have bruised a little."

"If he had music on, he wouldn't have heard anyone coming," Bethany said, "which explains why the back door could be broken noisily for the killer to gain entry, Len knowing sod all about it." She imagined that scenario and felt sick. Poor Len. "Okay, now we have a car to look for, we can—"

Her phone rang.

"Hi, Rob."

"You'll need to get down to fourteen Clarborough Road."

"Because?"

"Fran passed along the message about checking on Yasmin Lynch."

"And?" Her heart sank.

"She's dead."

CHAPTER FIFTEEN

Roland had all but shit himself seeing the police tent at Dullbourne. They'd found Daddy Len minus his testicles, and really, Roland should have walked back to his car and forgotten his mission, but the red mist had come down again, forcing him into the church. The vicar hadn't been of a mind to help him, and if the police weren't back there in the cemetery, Roland would have killed the bastard just for being awkward. Instead, he'd run to his car, and the idea to search online had landed in his head.

The internet café was always a godsend. For a few quid, you could browse to your heart's content, and Roland's heart was content once he'd settled in front of the screen in a café situated in a street behind the shopping centre. The search box, with 'Yasmin Lynch, Shadwell' in it, had revealed exactly where she lived. A stroke of luck, perhaps, but whatever it was, Roland was grateful. It saved trawling, digging deeper, getting frustrated at not being able to find what he wanted.

She ran her business from home, her address plain to see for Yasmin's Flower Creations, and he wondered if she'd made the MUM wreath that was at Julieanne's grave. Of course she had, and what a nice, personal touch that was, the fucking arse-licking pleb. He'd gleaned from the letter that Yasmin had lived with their mother, and he'd thought about after he'd killed his sister. He fancied poking through Mummy's belongings, taking a keepsake.

He drove to fourteen Clarborough Road, parking down the side of the house in the shadows. It might help to disguise his car a bit.

He walked round the back, a clean poncho covering his jacket, the hood over his head. The rain beat down as if the clouds had sucked up all the canals and rivers, then dumped it on Shadwell. He'd driven through a fair few puddles on his way over, and some of the roads were flooded at the sides.

Storms created such a mess.

He should know. Look what the storm inside him had done.

He knocked on the glass of the door, the thuds dull from his gloves, and waited. She appeared in the kitchen from the hallway, a replica of Julieanne, but younger, her eyes red-rimmed where she'd probably been crying after beating herself up for living her best life and ignoring their mother. A tool belt clung to her waist, tan leather. A packet of thin wire poked out from one of the two front pockets, and in the various loops hung scissors, pliers, and a Stanley knife.

He'd need to be careful then. If she got hold of those, she could hurt him more than she already had.

She cocked her head, frowning, probably asking herself why a stranger stood at her back door and not the front, with a poncho over his coat and black leather gloves on his clenched hands. He shrugged to show he meant no harm, when harm was all he intended. Yasmin came over and eyed him through the glass while turning the key, appearing wary, and he'd bet she thought: Who are you? What do you want?

A big skinny fool, she opened the door, reeling a little from the smack of wind, the driving rain, which entered her property as if it lived there. "Hello?"

Roland smiled and punched her in the face. She cried out, staggering backwards, arms flapping, her mouth morphing into a wiggly shape. She crashed into the dining table, one of the chairs toppling over to rest on its side. Hands up to her face, she stared at him between her slender, ring-decorated fingers. He stepped in and shut the door, advancing on her with murder on his mind, his fingers itching to grab her neck.

He launched a right hook at her temple, giving her a taste of the pain he'd endured throughout his life. She landed on her back on top of the table. Positioning himself between her scrawny legs, he pummelled her, hitting wherever he could, letting all the rage and jealousy out, the envy, the resentment, that fact that she'd had their mother right there and had squandered her presence, while he'd missed her, mourned her, desperate to see her again.

"You fucking ungrateful bitch," he said through gritted teeth. "You wasted your time with her; you didn't value her. She could have spent it with me, and I'd never have given her one ounce of loneliness. But you? You let her be by herself, alone, while you fucked off out getting pissed up with your friends, living your 'best life'."

Yasmin mumbled, whimpered, held her hands up in self-defence, blood on the backs of them where he'd walloped her and her nose had gushed. It looked broken. Like him. Like his heart.

He'd bite her face off in a minute if she tipped him over the edge.

Evil is the butcher.

"What was that?" he asked, still whacking her. "Lost your tongue now, have you? I can make that happen. Cut the fucker out."

She squealed and tried to get up.

He pressed her back down. "Did you think I wouldn't know? Wouldn't find out you existed? Did you both laugh about the son who was oblivious? Well, sister, you can fuck right off."

While he continued battering her, even once she'd gone limp and her breaths no longer wheezed, he thought about the spirit in the cedar tree, how it must have infected him after he'd transplanted it, burrowing inside him so he had the urge to kill. The neighbour had been right, death had come, but not to him, and not until years later, when he'd been old enough to do what he'd done to—

He stopped, gazing down at her, his poncho spattered with her blood, his gloves shiny with it, the light from the kitchen area showing up its red hue. His face was wet, the smell delightful.

"Now then, you." He took her Stanley knife out of her belt. "See what happens when you steal someone's mother? The cedar spirit comes for you."

Roland carved into her forehead, then made an X on each cheek, the blade going right through and creating four triangles that reminded him of the rubber tea towel holder they'd had stuck to the back of the kitchen cupboard door in Jamaica Street.

"Imagine taking a selfie now, eh?" He released his usual giggle, the one that came with a sweep of mania inside him that rushed through his veins. "Wouldn't you look a fucking state." He moved into the kitchen area and found tea towels in a drawer. Grabbing two, he stuffed the corners in her cheek flaps. "That's all you're good for now. A tea towel holder."

She stared, sightless, at the ceiling. No apology for him. No asking him if he was all right. Selfish, that was what she was, even in death.

He walked out into the rain, standing there on the patio so the water could wash all the redness off him. The dark slabs barely showed the pink fluid, then it was sluiced away by hard stabs of rain, ushering it along and down the cracks where the cement had crumbled.

Like he'd never been here.

He went back inside, stared at her mangled face for a bit, then, disgusted at her lack of reaction, he climbed the stairs, incensed that the biggest room was full of boxes. What a daughter Yasmin had turned out to be, packing all Mummy's stuff so quickly. He used the damp Stanley knife to rip open a box and dug out a pink jumper, soft wool, maybe cashmere. That'd do. At least he'd have something tangible that had belonged to her. He could sniff it and lick it and rub it on his face after he'd wiped a steak all over himself.

Downstairs, the jumper draped around his shoulders, the cuffs tied in a knot on his chest, he glared at Yasmin again, still so jealous of her. He ripped her T-shirt down the middle with the Stanley and jabbed the blade into her stomach. So many slits happened then, thickened blood oozing from each one, a mark for every year he'd been without Mummy.

Outside, he let the rain wash him once more, a perfect partner in crime this time, not a hindrance, not at all, and threw the Stanley indoors. It landed on the mess of that cow's stomach, and he sighed at a job well done, so pleased with himself it wasn't funny. The jumper got soaked, and that was annoying because it might wash away Mummy's smell.

In the car, he reversed out of the drive, watching for nosy neighbours. Someone was washing the inside of their windows, circular motions with scrunched newspaper, an old trick Daddy had told him about years ago when he'd taught Roland how to do it — "You're my dogsbody, son." He stared at her, willing her with his eyes to keep his visit to herself or he'd be back for her, giving her the Yasmin Treatment, and then he was out of there, heading towards home, the artic, where he'd climb in the cab and go to Abingdon, walk down Jamaica Street, and stand in front of the two-up, two-down, remembering, recalling everything, eventually shooed away by the woman who lived there now.

The woman who had his mother in the bottom of the garden beneath the cedar tree.

* * *

Roland didn't get to climb in the cab and drive away scot-free like he'd planned. As he sped along the road on the other side of the central dual carriageway barrier, glancing over at his lorry in the distance, parked where it was on the country lane, his stomach rolled over. Knots formed, boulder-like and heavy.

A police car sat behind it. An officer walked along, seemingly inspecting his home. Had they discovered who he was? Had he slipped up somewhere? Had killing two daddies in one place meant he'd pushed the boundaries?

It was too late to fix that now.

He continued on, coming to the roundabout at the top of the rise and taking one of the turnoffs that led to God knew where. He found a lay-by and parked, then took his binoculars from the glove box. Out of the car and across the road, under the cover of trees, he peered in the direction of his artic, zooming in. Spots of rain landed on the binocular lenses, the tears of the dead.

The copper reached to grab the cab door handle and haul himself up, nosing inside.

That was okay. He wouldn't see anything out of the ordinary. He might smell something, though, if he went too close to the rear doors, but maybe the wind would carry it away before there was a chance to get a whiff.

Roland was in a quandary. He could drive away now, leaving his home behind, and start again with a new one. He had enough money for that. The interest alone would buy an artic. But what about the mummies? If that officer went inside the back, he'd see them all, *and* Julieanne's innards all over the floor, *and* Daddy Len's bag of clothes in a black bag.

Shit.

And then the policeman jumped down, got in his car, and drove off.

Roland ran to the Fiat and slid in, swerved onto the tarmac, heading for the roundabout again. This time, he took the country road turning, stopped behind the artic, sorted the ramp, and put his car inside. He emptied his caravan loo tank contents outside, as he always did when leaving a lay-by, and jumped in the cab.

He checked his map for another out-of-the-way place he could park and went there, needing time to think. If he travelled to Jamaica Street now, after the policeman may have taken down the artic's registration number, he'd be caught in the one place he didn't want to be found, or even on the way there, seeing as speed cameras perched on the sides of roads, sneaky bastards on poles.

He needed new plates.

* * *

The pink jumper hung from a butcher's hook by its label, drying nicely beside Julieanne after he'd washed it. He wondered if she recognised it as hers.

He'd nipped to an ironmonger's shop to buy some black tape, making the three a B and the one a four, and decided the number plate was sufficiently disguised for now. He stood in the back of the artic at the new location and stared at the mummies, then at the floor in front of Julieanne. It was stained, covered in mess, a fly feasting on the pile of offal.

"You greedy little twat."

He waved to scare the fly and stuffed her innards into a black bag and popped it in the fridge, but really, he ought to get rid of it. Bad enough that a couple of other flies had got in her stomach hole and were buzzing around inside, settling from time to time, probably laying eggs or whatever it was they did when presented with so much to scoff. The maggots would come then — *Show me your maggot, boy* — and she'd be overrun with the buggers, all of them squirming about, falling from the cavity onto the floor, writhing there until he crushed them with his boots.

He liked doing that.

"Look at you all," he seethed at the mummies while washing his soiled hands. "What good are you to me? You just hang there or dance, and even then it's me pushing you that makes you do it, never of your own accord. You don't talk. You don't offer hugs — it's me who has to ask for them, begging for your attention."

He glared at Julieanne, the worst culprit, the mummy who didn't smell like the others, although that wasn't true anymore. With her inner flesh exposed, she had an aroma about her now that was pleasant to him; he'd enjoy sniffing it when he drove to Abingdon. He must be losing it if he'd only just noticed the tang — he could taste it in the air.

Had it filtered out to the copper? Was he planning on coming back with reinforcements? Roland laughed. The artic wasn't at that spot anymore, so more fool them.

Julieanne's sticker smile taunted him, and he went along the row. No point bothering with Jen at the moment, seeing as her flesh was at that wonderful disgusting stage, but Julieanne's and Angela's, and Susan's, and Geraldine's and Lucy's smiles, he took them all away, and from those other, earlier dried-out crusty bitches down the end by Mummy's chair.

In his car, he drew new mouths, all downturned, sad. He pressed them in place on those they'd stick to and paced in front of the hanging mums.

"That's better. You're all upset. You're all sorry you had a Yasmin. Serves yourselves right that she's dead. Now it's only me left. The one you *should* have cared about."

She left you, son. Didn't love you. Only I love you, and don't I show it at night?

Daddy hadn't lied after all. She *had* left, and what Roland had seen in the back garden was just his childish imagination, his hopes, his dreams that she was there, down in the flowerbed. Julieanne moving on and having Yasmin was proof that Roland had just been kidding himself, and the letter had confirmed it.

As for Yasmin, what was it she'd written?

We'll meet again one day, and I swear we'll spend all those missed times together, catching up . . .

Well, she'd be searching for Julieanne to catch up now all right — or she would if Julieanne was even in Heaven, but she wasn't, she was here, looking all chastised and dejected, as she should. Yasmin could wander the halls of the afterlife all she wanted, she'd never find her mother.

My mother.

And he should have told her just that, right before he'd killed her, the mother-hogging little cow.

He should move on. He should get away from Shadwell and never come back. But his ire was up, his thirst for killing another daddy strong. Voices in his head told him not to believe Daddy, and confusion swirled around in there. What was the truth? He didn't know anymore. Daddy? The Enlightenment? Yasmin's letter?

Daddy's the liar.

He gripped his head and squeezed as if that would make him see what to do.

It did.

Roland couldn't drive away.

How could he leave when Daddy Volton was still alive?

* * *

At eighteen, Roland knew things weren't right at home. As in, properly knew. For all of his childhood after Mummy had gone, he'd been uneasy, realising things weren't how they were supposed to be, but he'd put up with it because it was all he knew.

That was what abused kids did, according to Oprah.

A chance conversation in the pub one night, the pub at the end of Jamaica Street, which stood beside the little shop, had Roland spilling out his story to a stranger who'd been eager to listen while Roland plied him with booze. Except Roland had made out it was a friend of his those things had happened to, and the father wasn't Daddy but another man.

"That's sick," the bloke, Teddy, said. "No kid should go through that. Your mate knows that's not normal, yeah?"

"He didn't think it was, but his dad told him he'd better not say anything if he knew what was good for him."

"Who licks their kid like that, though? Who touches him down there? And as for all the other shit he had to do to the dad . . . Sick, that's what it is. And what's with that licking anyway?"

"The dad said his uncle used to do it to him, got him to lick meat for some reason an' all, and it was just something you did to little boys.

You know, passed the horror on." Roland shrugged, like he was just relating a sorry tale, nothing to do with him.

"No, it isn't something you do to boys, not unless you're a fucking nonce." Teddy shook his head. "That's stealing a childhood, that is. Messing your friend up. No one has the right to do that." He sipped his pint, the froth from the bitter latching on to his top lip. "How's your mate now?" He licked it off.

"Confused."

"I bet. I'd kill my old man if he did that to me, wouldn't you?"

"Dunno."

But he did know. He got Teddy even more sloshed so he'd have trouble remembering their conversation, remembering him, and went home, thinking of ways to kill Daddy so he wouldn't get the blame. It'd have to look like suicide, and apart from an overdose of tablets Roland didn't have, maybe he could slit Daddy's wrist.

He entered the house, and Daddy was up waiting, as usual, ready for the licking, for Roland's maggot. He used Roland worse on these nights, saying he had to be rough because the alcohol would deaden Roland's senses. But this was the end of it, he wouldn't take anymore, and while he was afraid of his father, while he should have just packed his stuff and left ages ago, a perverse thread kept him tethered to a man who'd done what Teddy had said: stolen his childhood. And his innocence, his mother, his sense of worth.

Roland followed Daddy upstairs after sliding a knife up his jumper sleeve. He had an idea on the way, of switching things up, letting Daddy think he was well into it, taking some kind of control, as if he enjoyed what he was put through.

Daddy's face showed surprise at Roland's suggestion, for Roland to sit propped against the headboard, Daddy between his legs facing away from him.

"I can play with you then," Roland said, "and we'd both get to watch."

Daddy smiled at that.

They stripped and got into position, Roland's jumper on the bed beside them, the knife waiting inside that sleeve to come out and do some damage. Daddy got himself excited, so Roland pulled the knife out and, with Daddy's right hand busy, Roland quickly drew the blade down the inside of Daddy's left arm.

It took a moment for the hot blood to register for Daddy, the pain of the slice, and he stopped fumbling to stare across at his arm bleeding a waterfall. Roland remained where he was, holding both Daddy's wrists down, curling his legs around his father's to pin them. All the while his abuser struggled, sobbing, panicking with every second his life drained out of him.

"Am I a wimp now? Have I grown some balls?" Roland whispered, his mouth on the king of pig's ear. He ached to bite it off.

Daddy didn't answer.

Roland stayed there for a long time afterwards, the dead weight heavy, Daddy's head lolling to one side, the back of his head warm on Roland's chest. Then he got out from beneath him and positioned the body, careful not to get blood transfer from him to anywhere else. He stared at his hand. It had red on it, and he created the same pattern with some seeping blood on Daddy's hand, then cleaned the knife handle of prints and placed it in Daddy's curled fingers, pressing so his palm print transferred.

Crimson tinted the blade.

In the shower, Roland whistled, washed all the evidence away, bleaching the bath afterwards. The cedar spirit settled inside him when he climbed into bed, and he slept right through until morning, where he got up and dressed, went into Daddy's room to pick up his own clothes. He put a load of washing on, made breakfast, and ate it alone, without Daddy there to talk about the previous night, dissecting it, ensuring Roland lived through it all over again.

Nice and peaceful. No stress. No shame.

Roland started work at the shop at nine, and Daddy usually arrived about half seven, opening at eight thirty for those who wanted to buy stuff on the way to taking kids to school. Roland turning up and finding the shop locked meant customers outside would see him.

Good.

He walked there and, sure enough, a line of six ladies stood waiting.

"We've been here for twenty-five minutes now," one said. "The blinds aren't even up, look." She pointed to the striped efforts covering the front door and window.

"He's probably gone to the meat man. He generally collects goods today." Keys out, Roland unlocked the door and entered, disabling the alarm.

The women followed, standing in a queue, and he supposed they were waiting for him to sort their meat. He got to work taking the loaded trays out of the back fridge — Roland always restocked them the night before — and placed them in the glass counter, switching it on so the base got cold. Next, he dealt with the till float, then served the gaggle.

"I didn't hear him leave this morning," Roland said. "I had a few bevvies last night so only woke up when my alarm went off."

"You saying he usually goes to the meat man," a grey-haired harridan said. "Well, he usually opens up then goes after you've arrived at nine."

Roland shrugged. "Maybe he changed his mind today."

He left it until lunchtime before he locked the shop and returned home, hanging the washing out then 'finding' Daddy, seeing the blood as if for the first time, and getting himself into a mock panic, rushing down to the phone in the hallway to ring the police. So many questions when they arrived, and Roland answered them all while crying and shaking on the outside, laughing and celebrating inside.

"Killed himself," an officer announced, coming down the stairs and giving Roland a look of sympathy once he reached him at the bottom. "Slit his arm."

"Oh God . . ."

They were in the house for ages, those coppers. Roland spoke to them, then some bloke in a suit had gone through it all again.

No, Roland hadn't seen his dad when he'd got home from the pub; he'd assumed he'd gone to bed.

No, he hadn't been up this morning until half eight so hadn't seen him then either.

No, he hadn't been too worried about his father not being at work because he usually went to the meat fella today and could have got held up. He'd only worried by lunchtime, so had phoned the supplier, who'd said he hadn't turned up. Roland had gone home, as he usually did, to hang the washing out and put another load on. That was why he'd found his father — he'd gone in the bedroom to get his laundry.

"Terrible business," Suit Man said. "Just terrible."

No, it wasn't terrible. It was perfect and wonderful and freeing.

No more maggots. No more licks. No more Daddy.

CHAPTER SIXTEEN

Bethany and Mike stood in the kitchen and stared across into the dining area at the body. The state of Yasmin Lynch knotted her stomach. The killer had gone at her with a blade, her flat stomach littered with slices of differing lengths, her cheeks cut, the corner ends of tea towels wedged into them. Was that significant? Did it mean something? From Bethany's viewpoint, it meant sod all and was probably a move by the killer for whatever reason, or one to throw them off, get them wondering about it, wasting their time while he got away.

This was pure rage, the way she'd been killed. Personal. The word BITCH stood out on her forehead, despite the layer of blood on the rest of the skin. Puffa — and it had to be him — had taken the time to carve it there, unaware that officers were en route while he'd been doing it. He'd thought he had plenty of time.

He had a thing about his mother being a bitch. Was he deluded and thought Yasmin *was* his mother? Did Angela Lockwood and Julieanne Lynch now have this word on *their* foreheads, wherever he'd taken them?

She'd had a call from Fran on the way over here, and Mike had put it on speaker. Officers in Manchester were putting an exhumation order through for a Susan Gorman, the only lady to be buried in Gowly village on the day a butcher went missing from there. High Peak Borough Council had cordoned off the grave already, and family members were being spoken to.

How awful to have someone ask if they could dig your loved one's grave to check if she was actually in there.

Despite years passing between then and now, a cemetery attendant, when questioned, recalled seeing a man matching Puffa's description loitering about after Susan's funeral — he'd attended it, left at one point, then came back — and she'd asked him to move along when he'd been there for an hour acting oddly. Normally, she allowed mourners to remain for as long as they wanted up until she closed the gates, but he'd taken to running around in between graves, laughing manically, and had no care that people had been laid to rest beneath his feet, not to mention he'd trampled some flowers. He'd also hugged a cedar tree, which was weird, shouting, "Spirit, you are in me and I am you."

Bloody nutter.

What had pushed the police forward with the exhumation was the attendant mentioning Susan's grave had settled 'funny', the mud not just dipping as one large rectangle but in several different places within it. She'd put it down to the rain clumping the mud in sections, but once the police had told her what was going on in Shadwell, she'd realised what had really happened.

"This man needs locking up and the key throwing away," Mike said. "And if the Manchester butcher is found in Susan's grave, with Susan missing, the question is, where are all the stolen bodies? What if he drives off to the next town or city and buries them in other fresh plots after he's done whatever he's doing to them?"

"That's too many exhumations to think about. Already, there are ten missing butchers bar Dave and Len, so I'd say there are ten other ladies who have been taken. That's enough, let alone more to check if some have two people in them."

"I don't get why he's even taking them. What's the point if he only wants to bury butcher body parts? I'd just dig down enough to hide them then cover the bags up."

"God knows. What I want to know is, why come here after Yasmin? What has she got to do with this? Did she know him? Did Julieanne? We know he wasn't aware of the address from what the vicar said, so he found it somehow. The back and front doors haven't been broken into, so she must have let him in — the back door is unlocked. Why would you allow a stranger inside your home?"

"You wouldn't, ordinarily, but given those cuts on her, she may not have had much choice. He could have slashed her face to incapacitate her, then forced his way in."

Bethany's attention was drawn from the body to Isabelle coming through from the hallway.

"Everything appears normal upstairs, apart from one packing box being slit open," Isabelle said. "The box is damp where it's been cut, so make of that what you will. The contents may be Julieanne's things. Perhaps Yasmin decided to take something out just before she was killed."

"Damp? A wet knife was used?" Bethany frowned.

Isabelle shrugged. "Beats me. In the back bedroom, there's a working area. She must have been in the middle of creating a wreath, because a wire frame has been made, and a few flowers are attached. The rest are beside it. Also, there are business cards for a company, Yasmin's Flower Creations, with this address on them. So, he knocks, she comes down to answer, and this happens." She pointed at Yasmin.

"Seems that's the way of it." Bethany sighed. "And it explains why she let him in if she runs her business from here. I wonder why he didn't strangle her like Dave and Len?"

"The murder weapon is on her stomach — it's obvious those are Stanley cuts — and she has other tools on her belt, so I'm guessing he stabbed her with her own implement." Isabelle moved back to stand in front of the cooker. "The weapons are right there, so maybe he just grabbed one and got to work. Or it could be escalation. He strangles Dave, stabs and strangles Len, then just stabs Yasmin, along with beating her up. The use of a weapon with Len could have pushed him to try what it was like to kill this way, have a go at something new. We could stand here yakking all day and never come up with the answer. Some things just 'are'. They happen, no explanation. The end result is, she's dead — and still warmish. That Stanley is clean, which means it was washed prior to being placed on her."

"So it could have been wet, used on the box upstairs," Mike said.

Bethany nodded, thinking of everything they needed to do.

Uniforms were in the street questioning the neighbours, and she decided to join them while waiting for Presley to turn up. She left the house and strolled across the road in her protectives, to PC Penny Dickens, who chatted with a lady on her doorstep opposite. She wouldn't normally butt in, would usually wait for Penny to finish, except the neighbour seemed agitated and kept gesturing at Yasmin's house.

Bethany held out her ID and stood beside Penny. "DI Bethany Smith. Everything okay?"

"No, it bloody well isn't," the neighbour said.

"What's your name, please?"

"Holli Ballard." She folded her arms. "Look, I was just telling her that I saw a bloke leaving Yasmin's. He got into a green Fiat. Well shifty, he was. He turned up when I'd just sprayed Windolene — the dog gets his wet nose all over the glass — so I didn't get a look at his face to begin with. A bit later, after I'd let my windows soak, I came back to wipe it off with newspaper. Anyway, he gets in his car, down the side of her house, it was, and reverses, looking around like he wanted to see if he'd been spotted. He stared right at me, the creepy git, and what am I meant to do about that now?"

"How do you mean?" Bethany asked.

"Well, you've got those bloody Scene of Crime people there, haven't you, so something's happened. What if he comes back for me, to shut me up because I saw him? Happens on the telly all the time."

Bethany took her phone out and held Puffa's image up. "This him?"

"Yes, and he's weird as anything. He had one of those ponchos on, transparent."

"Was it dirty?"

"Not that I noticed."

"What did he have on underneath it?"

"A black coat."

Not grey? "What kind of coat?"

"What? I have no idea, I wasn't close enough, plus it was raining, which fuzzed up the view. Blue jeans, though. Boots. Oh, and he had something pink draped over his shoulders."

Pink?

Had he put the poncho on as protective clothing? He'd have been covered in blood, so had the rain washed it off or had Holli just not been able to see it?

"That's very helpful, thank you."

"What's even more helpful is I took the number plate down."

Bethany's heart sped up. She glanced at Penny, who shrugged. Holli clearly hadn't mentioned the registration number to her.

"Can we have that then, please?" Bethany asked.

Holli gave it, and Bethany tapped it out into her message app and sent it to Rob: RUN THIS VEHICLE, PLEASE.

"How long would you say he was in Yasmin's for?" Penny asked.

"Time enough for me to boil a half-filled kettle and make a cuppa." Holli turned to her window. "That dog's at it again, messing up the glass. Get down, Shadow!"

The German shepherd smiled then disappeared.

"Good guard dog?" Bethany asked.

"Soft as anything, but he'd bite your arm off if you broke in." Holli shivered. "So it's not so bad if that man . . . God, I don't even want to think about it."

"He came from round the back of Yasmin's when he left. Did he enter that way?" Bethany asked.

She caught sight of the neighbour to the left of Holli's, who nosed outside, eyes wide.

Holli shook her head. "I didn't see him at the front door."

"Okay, I'll leave you with Penny so she can get everything written down." Bethany walked down the path then up the next one. The door opened as she raised her hand to knock. "Hi, my name's DI Bethany Smith, and I'm here about an incident at Yasmin Lynch's over the road." She presented her ID then slipped it away again. "Did you see anything within the last two hours?"

"Not from here, no, but I was next door to Yasmin's having a cuppa with old Glenda in number fifteen. She's gone for her aquatherapy now — well, it's me who takes her; I just got back — so she won't be able to tell you anything until later."

"And your name is?"

"Cassie Exline."

"Okay, Cassie, were you at Glenda's when a male visited Yasmin?"

"I didn't know it was a man until I looked out from behind Glenda's nets in the kitchen. The fences between the houses over the road are diamond wire, about waist height, so you can see into everyone's gardens. I sat at the table with Glenda, having a coffee, and I thought I heard something crash and Yasmin cry out. The thing is, with the rain hammering down and whacking the window, it was difficult to know if I'd really heard anything. Plus, Yasmin's been crying a lot since Julieanne died — Glenda hears her at night mainly — so I put it down to that. Grief."

"You mentioned seeing him though the nets."

"Yes, I noticed movement in the back garden so got up to have a look. Julieanne and Yasmin don't have men calling, so it bothered me when I saw one standing on the patio. He had a poncho on and stood there getting wet. I thought it was weird, but at the same time none of my business, and when he went back indoors, I sat down again. I could still see into Yasmin's garden so kept an ear cocked for more noise and an eye peeled for him coming back out. I definitely heard him going up the stairs, or it could have been Yasmin, then he was in the garden again, this time with a pink jumper tied round his neck, over the poncho. It's Julieanne's jumper, so it stood out as off that he had it on."

"Yes, that's definitely strange, especially over the poncho in this weather."

Had the jumper been in the packing box?

Cassie shivered. "He moved out of my sight, so when I heard a car start, I walked through to the front room and watched — Glenda stayed in the dining area. She's got bad knees, hence the aquatherapy. He left in a green car, I don't know the make, sorry, and he slowed slightly outside Holli's as he drove past, then he sped up and was gone. I took Glenda to aqua, and when I got back, a copper was here, knocking on Yasmin's door." She winced. "I just put it down to Yasmin having an argument then calling the police. I made a bite to eat, ate it, came back into my lounge, and saw you talking to Holli." She stared across at Yasmin's. "Something's happened, hasn't it."

Bethany nodded. "I'm afraid so. Do you know of anyone who would want to hurt Yasmin?"

"God, no. Nice young lady. Always smiling."

"What about Julieanne?"

"Oh, she was the loveliest."

"So you know of no one who would want to disturb her grave?"

"Bloody hell, no! I saw it online while I was eating . . . someone was removed from a grave at Wallflower."

Peter Uxbridge has got wind of it. "Yes, and at Dullbourne, too. Julieanne."

"God, the news article didn't mention that. It did say about Dave the butcher, though. So why . . . What's happened to Yasmin?"

"I'm sorry to say she's been murdered, probably by the man you saw." She kept Len out of it, not wanting to freak the woman out even more than she already was.

Cassie flapped her hand in front of her face as if that info was too much. "Oh God . . ."

Bethany's phone blipped, and she smiled at Cassie. "I have to go. Thanks for your time. I'll send Penny here next to take a statement. She's the PC out the front."

She sorted that with Penny then walked to the SOCO van, opened one of the back doors, and stuck her head inside to shield her phone from the rain.

Rob: THE FIAT'S LAST OWNER IS A MRS SALLY BARNES IN SURREY, BUT SHE SOLD THE CAR TO A GENTLEMAN SIX MONTHS AGO. SAID GENTLEMAN HASN'T REGISTERED IT IN HIS NAME.

Bethany: SO SOMEONE WANTS TO STAY OFF THE RADAR.

Rob: SEEMS SO, BUT SHE DID SAY HE'D LEARNT ABOUT HER CAR BEING FOR SALE WHILE THEY WERE AT HER FRIEND'S FUNERAL. SHE HAD A SIGN IN THE WINDOW ADVERTISING IT, AND HE ASKED HER ABOUT IT. PAID HER IN CASH LATER THAT AFTERNOON.

At a funeral. Fucking hell.

Bethany: DID YOU FIND OUT WHOSE FUNERAL IT WAS?

Rob: I DID. A LAURA CHESSOP.

Bethany: OKAY, GET ON TO THE POLICE THERE AND TELL THEM HER NAME. THEY ALREADY KNOW ABOUT THIS INQUIRY AS A BUTCHER WENT MISSING IN THAT AREA — FRAN'S GOT THE LIST OF LOCATIONS IF YOU NEED IT. YOU CAN BET IF HE WAS AT THAT FUNERAL, THERE'S A BUTCHER'S REMAINS IN LAURA'S GRAVE.

Rob: CHRIST. ON IT NOW.

Bethany rushed back into Yasmin's. "Mike, we have the number plate for the Fiat, but the man who bought it hasn't registered it as his, so no address for him. What a sodding surprise." She went on to explain everything. "The cheeky git bought a car from the deceased's friend, and he knew damn well he'd be going to that grave later after killing a butcher, probably using that car."

"Sick shit. He's got no conscience, obviously." Mike sighed.

Her phone warbled again, this time as a call.

"Yep, Fran?"

"Hi. Tammy has come off CCTV now as it's yielded nothing, but she did find something else that might be of interest. Considering butchers are a theme, we were chatting about the possible reasons they're a target. Why people kill certain others, that sort of thing."

Bethany tapped her foot: *Love you loads, Fran, but get on with it, will you?*

"Okay, so she suggested looking for butchers who have died, not just gone missing, and there are a few. Anyway, all but one have plausible deaths — heart attack, stroke, whatever. This one man, a Lee Didsbrough, committed suicide, cutting his wrist. So Tammy phoned up the station that dealt with it, explained why she was calling, and she was put through to this DCI who was a DS at the time, and he said that while suicide was ruled, he'd always had his doubts. Said the son had sold up the business as soon as possible, the family home, too, and buggered off. The son is a Roland Didsbrough — no social media whatsoever. Want me to get the go-ahead to run a check on his monetary footprint? I've already searched for him, and his last fixed abode was eighteen Jamaica Street, Abingdon, with nothing since. An old lady lives there now and has done since Roland sold it to her."

"Right, yes, get the financial check sorted. One of you ring the woman, see if she had any direct contact with this Roland. See if she's old enough that she doesn't have a phone or email — we could do with her viewing his picture. If that's an issue, ring Thames Valley and get them to go round there and show it to her."

"Okay, I'll phone you back in a bit."

Bethany looked from Isabelle to Mike. "We have a possible name for Puffa, thanks to Tammy going the extra mile." She told them what she'd done. "So while we *do* have a potential identity, it seems he hasn't lived anywhere at all since he sold his father's house."

"So it's someone out on the road, like we thought," Mike said.

Her phone rang again. "Interesting. It's Glen Underby." She answered it. "What have you got for me?"

"A few of us have been out looking for lorries. Now, I saw one on the lane parallel to the dual carriageway out of Shadwell, but the driver wasn't in the cab, nor in the little bed above, so the only place he could have been is in the back. I did knock but got no answer. Nothing seemed amiss except for a strange smell, and I put it down to a dead animal nearby, a wild one. I drove off, and it was bugging me, the dead animal theory. So I went back there, and the lorry was gone. What remained was a faint smell, and so I had a look at the grass verge. There's fluid here — I'm at the scene now — seeping into the grass, plus a small patch of it on gravel.

It's pink. What else is weird, is someone's dumped a load of excrement, which wasn't there the first time I came."

"Ooer. How much excrement are we talking?"

"Days' worth. Like, a big pile of it."

"Okay . . . I'll let Isabelle know, and she'll send someone out to you. Hang tight. Actually, cordon that verge off."

"Will do. I rang the plate in to Rob the first time, by the way, and it came back as last belonging to a haulage firm in Bedford. They'd sent it to scrap, so it seems someone bought it from there. Rob said the scrapyard has shut down, the owner deceased, so that's not going to do us any good."

"Thanks. Do the cordon, then go and sit in your car and lock the doors. Chat soon."

Bethany frowned, cut the call, and related what Glen had said.

"A pile of *shit*?" Mike asked.

"I'm more bothered about the pink fluid." Isabelle left the room and called up the stairs. Her voice carried through. "Can two of you do me a favour and go to another location, please?"

Bethany raised her eyebrows at Mike. "I'm thinking a caravan and the owner dumped his crap out, but Glen says it was a lorry."

"Maybe there's a Portaloo in there for long-haul journeys. Might not be anything sinister. Well, apart from the pink fluid."

"And the smell of a rotting animal." She sighed. "So this fella we're after lives nowhere. How the hell are we going to find him? He could have fucked off after killing Yasmin. Let's face it, that's obviously what he's done if that's his lorry."

Isabelle came back in. "Right, two of my lot have just gone there. Not much else we can do on that but wait and see if the fluid is human blood. I rang Aradul to warn him we'll need a rush on that when he gets the specimen. If the killer's washed all the blood off him from this scene on the verge, it could be Yasmin's and a tie to that location — and the fact a lorry was parked there matches our trucker theory."

"But what about the Fiat?" Bethany didn't get this at all. She rang Glen. "Hi, I know I said stay in your car, but can you get out for a sec and check that gravel you mentioned. Look behind where the lorry was parked and see if there are tyre marks consistent with a car."

"Hang on, I didn't even get in the car yet. Just finishing the cordon." Rustling sounded, maybe him tying it off, then the crunch of gravel. "Ah, yes. Quite a few leading up to the back of the lorry, as if someone's come and gone several times, but they stop about a car length away from it. There are lines in the gravel, deep, as if something pressed against it."

"Cheers. Go back to the car."

She put her phone in her pocket. "Lorries have ramps, yes?"

Mike and Isabelle nodded.

"Strong enough for a Fiat to drive up it and into the back?" She tapped her fingers on her arm.

"Bugger me," Mike said. "So he uses the Fiat while in whatever town or city but drives the lorry to each location?"

"It's plausible, isn't it?" She got her phone back out and messaged Fran.

> Bethany: RING AROUND HOTELS AND TRAVEL LODGES IN SHADWELL TO SEE IF ANY MALE STAYED THERE WITH THE FOLLOWING NUMBER PLATE — SOME PLACES REQUIRE IT FOR PARKING.

She sent the one for the Fiat. "He could leave the lorry and stay in hotels, so I've just asked Fran to check that."

"Right, but what if he hasn't stayed anywhere?" Mike furrowed his brow. "He could kip in his car or even the bed in the lorry cab. It wouldn't be classed as unusual. Truckers do that all the time."

"Best to go down all avenues," Isabelle said. "With no fixed address, we're basically pissing in the wind."

"Such an undelightful term." Presley walked in, protectives on, and scowled at the floor. "Only one evidence step when there's so much blood?"

"Oh, bog off, mate." Isabelle moved to the kitchen doorway. "Can we have some more steps in here, please?" She went and stood by the sink unit. "As you could quite clearly see when you came in, we weren't near the body anyway, and when we were, we took it in turns to use the step. Now, if that's your only grumble . . . ?"

A SOCO entered and placed four steps down.

Presley, ignoring her, approached the body and stared at it, shaking his head. "Looks like she was beaten to death. The stab wounds aren't deep enough to be the cause. They're slices rather than stabs, so more of a mutilation than an intent to kill. But the beating, that's intention. An angry person. Not often fists are down as a murder weapon, but I'd say this is the case here." He got on with taking the temperature. "Within the last two hours."

Bethany nodded. "That marries with the info I got from the neighbours. Leona said she'd get back to me with any CCTV for this area, and she hasn't, so I'm assuming the estate only has it at the row of shops."

Isabelle arched her eyebrows then gave Presley's back a pointed stare. "Like I said, pissing in the wind."

Presley tutted. Isabelle smirked. And Bethany? She said goodbye and left. They needed to see that verge.

CHAPTER SEVENTEEN

Roland sat in his car outside the internet café and stared down the road at the back of the precinct. Volton was in his yard area, using a brush to sweep up. He'd just had a delivery, and bits of packing stuff had fallen from the lorry onto the ground.

Volton had too many employees for Roland to get at him inside the shop, and he was taking a risk as it was, being so close. There were bound to be cameras out here, the shopping centre so up to date with security. A horrible guard had asked him to leave last time, and all he'd been doing was playing with his balls.

Roland reached over and took a clean poncho from his glove box, put it on, along with a beanie hat, then drew a smile on a sticker and slapped it over his mouth. That would have to do as a disguise. He'd kill Volton right there behind the shop. He couldn't chop him up without tools, but he had a penknife and could remove the testicles, which was the main thing. Some high-pitched giggles had snuck out of him on his way here, so he needed his manly food to keep the weird laughter at bay.

He got out of the Fiat and ran into Volton's yard, his tread near silent. The butcher, that fucking daddy, had his back to Roland, so with one well-aimed fist, Roland whacked the back of the man's neck. An *oof*, then Daddy went down on his knees, reaching to press a palm on his neck. Roland walloped him in the temple, and Daddy arced to one side, then righted himself. He didn't even turn to see who was attacking him, nor did he attempt to get up, so Roland whipped his lever from his pocket and jabbed it into the same place as Daddy Len, only deeper, the tool half embedded.

Daddy shouted out, something like, "Oh, fuck me, that *hurts*."

Roland ran round and kicked him in the face. Daddy fell backwards, landing on the lever, and his eyes, so wide, his mouth, so gaping, was the expression Roland had wanted to see. The lever had gone deeper, the end poking through Daddy's throat beside his quivering Adam's apple. And the blood, so much of it, spurted around the weapon to the beat of his disgusting, abusive heart.

Glancing around, Roland grinned behind the sticker smile, and Daddy stared, his hand fluctuating beside the lever. Blood dribbled and bubbled from between his lips, sputters joining this wonderful death party, groans and sounds of immense pain. And right in that moment, Roland sensed the eye of a camera on him, watching, repulsed by this show.

Penknife out of his pocket, he knelt and slashed at Daddy's thin trousers, through his boxers, until the jewels he sought were on full display. He lifted the maggot and cut the sac, unable to be careful and enjoy the task because . . . time. It wasn't on his side. A quick flick of the blade, and the man-food broke free, blood going everywhere, Daddy choking out incoherent words, and if he was saying sorry for what he'd done for years, if he was apologising for killing and burying Mummy, for the stripes, the Punishment, the licks, the maggot touching, the forced testicle eating, he wasn't sorry enough for Roland. No amount of explaining would cut it.

"You're a monster," he said to the butcher. "Evil."

And what are you?

Roland ignored that and shoved the warm, wet balls in his coat pocket. "Now fuck off to Hell."

It felt wrong walking away, not chopping him into pieces and putting him in Mummy's grave, like he was doing something terribly wrong, not staying true to his plan. A giggle from nerves crept out, and oh God, it sounded so feminine that he couldn't wait. He snatched a testicle out and bit into it, tearing off a mouthful, chewing, gagging, the damn thing refusing to break up into pieces. He swallowed the clump, got in his car, and rammed the other piece into his mouth, driving off towards home, that safe haven in the back of the artic. He struggled to eat again and had to gulp it down, waiting for the manliness to fill him.

There it was, a rush of feelings, and he laughed on purpose to see how it sounded. Deep, from the belly, a bloke's bellow.

Calm stole over him upon seeing his lorry. Fiat parked inside, he washed his hands and face, stripped off the poncho, and took the black bag of Julieanne's innards out of the fridge. He stuffed the poncho inside, then dumped the bag and the one containing Daddy Len's clothing out on the verge.

Time to move on.

He settled in the cab and inspected the map. There was a caravan park near here, so he'd go there and finally top up his water tanks. Jamaica Street was calling, that stretch of time where he didn't do bad things and wasn't this . . . this thing Daddy and the cedar spirit had created. He was that man talking to Teddy in the pub, confused about his upbringing, the abuse, and wanting someone on his side, to believe in him.

Engine rumbling, he pulled out of the lay-by.

Checked the rearview mirror.

A police car. Right up his arse, lights flashing.

CHAPTER EIGHTEEN

Bethany couldn't do much at the verge. SOCO had taken pictures and swabs, bagged the shit, and were measuring the tyre tracks and the lines in the beige gravel. She now drove back towards Shadwell, Mike resting his head on the rain-spattered window, his eyes closed.

Her phone rang, and she glanced across at her partner. He took it out of the cup holder and answered it on speaker.

"Mike here. Bethany's driving."

"It's Rob. We've got patrol chasing a lorry."

"Where?"

"On the dual carriageway heading south — the road next to where the excrement was dumped."

Bethany continued in that direction and put her foot down, heart galloping.

"What's the story?" she asked.

"Tory Yates was parked behind some bushes, monitoring the artic because the plate is so similar to the one Glen noted. She said a number and letter didn't look like the standard type, so it got her curiosity up. Then she spotted the green Fiat and rang me to match that plate. It's the same, so she waited as I was about to send backup. The driver put the car inside the artic, lobbed a couple of black bags on the verge, then drove off. She pursued. Another patrol has joined from farther down the road — it's waiting for the artic to come along. The driver is failing to stop, despite Tory having her lights and siren on."

"It's got to be him then," Mike said.

Bethany belted down the road, switching her own blues and siren on, bypassing cars that slowed to get out of her way.

Rob gave them the lorry plate number, and Mike sat forward, peering ahead to catch sight of it. No lorries, only cars. But hang on . . . was that a lorry in the distance? She couldn't tell because of the misty rain.

"Location, please?" Bethany asked, conscious of the wet surface.

"Just taking a turnoff, left, going onto the roundabout with roads to Shadwell and Hepley."

"I see it," she said, the lorry gunning it up the slip road, Tory close behind.

Bethany drove faster, adrenaline flooding her system. She covered the distance in seconds, then she was scooting up the slip and . . . "Fucking hell!"

The artic bounded onto the roundabout, a second police car coming from the right narrowly missing its back end. Tory followed, then the lorry leant to the left, the whole thing falling in slow motion then crashing onto the tarmac. Tyres screeched, Tory executed an emergency stop, and Bethany did the same, grabbing her phone and vaulting out of the car towards the lorry cab. A man climbed out through the driver's window, and she trained her focus on him as he jumped down and ran. Tory gave chase with Bethany, Mike coming abreast of them.

"Police! Stop!" Mike shouted.

The man pelted down the road that led to Shadwell.

Bethany yelled into her phone, "Crash, crash, crash. Suspect is on the run on Shadwell bypass, heading into the trees." She lost visuals on him for a moment, then, through the tree trunks, spotted him again, legging it across a field.

Bethany, Tory, and Mike lunged after him, Mike gaining faster, going ahead of them. He was maybe three or four steps behind the man, so he put on a burst of speed and reached out, grabbing his coat collar. The man snarled, an almost-caught animal, and shook Mike off. Mike stumbled, slipping on the soaked grass, and Tory raced on, her slim figure streaking forward. Then she was on him, tackling the fucker, the rain hammering on them, and they were down on the ground, Tory clinging to his back, the suspect giving it his all in bucking her off. Mike reached them, and he sank to his knees, grabbing the man's wrists and pinning them at the bottom of his back.

Tory cuffed him, saying, "I'm using restraints for our safety. You appear dangerous, therefore, you need to be secured."

Bethany slowed, her lungs burning, her throat on fire, sweat and rain coating her face.

She stopped and bent over, one hand braced on her knees, and sucked in long breaths. Phone raised to her ear, she said breathlessly, "Suspect apprehended." She gave Rob their location.

"Got it," he said. "A call's just come in from patrol at the lay-by. Looks like innards and a poncho inside a black bag, clothes in another."

Bloody hell . . . "Right. Get hold of Isabelle. I'm out." She jammed her phone away.

Mike and Tory hauled the bloke to his feet, and Bethany straightened to her full height and stared at the blood-smeared face of a killer, the skin around his mouth red raw. It was Puffa in all his ugly, frightening glory, and she acknowledged the frisson of fear that went through her as his gaze pierced into her. He wasn't right, that much was clear. Mad eyes. Evil mouth.

Where had that blood come from at the corners of his lips?

"Roland Didsbrough?" she asked, panting, hating the fact she showed weakness after chasing him — she needed to get fitter.

"How do you fucking know?" he barked, a frown contorting his strange features. He tried to shuck Mike and Tory off but failed, snarling in anger.

"You are under arrest for evading the police after you've been asked to pull over, for the suspicion of murder, and removing bodies from graves. You do not have to say anything . . ." She continued with the spiel, watching him closely.

His face paled, and his mouth flapped; it was clear he was trying to think of something to say. Then his features changed, softening, and he almost looked afraid. "This isn't my fault. None of it is. Ask the cedar spirit. It made me do this."

What? "I don't know what you're talking about, and I'm not interested in any bloody spirit." *Ah, the cemetery attendant in Manchester mentioned him hugging a cedar tree.*

"Daddy deserved this. Mummy did, too." Rain doused his head, the hair coming through a couple of millimetres long — no time to shave it?

Too busy killing. "No one deserved what you did to them," she bit out, rage rising. "No one deserved to be killed or dug up. If you think you can blame it on some spirit, you're very much mistaken. It was you, mate. *You.*" She yearned to hurt him, to shove her fingertips into his weird round eyes and gouge them out. *Calm down. Move it along.* "Why have you got blood on your face?"

"Testicles." His wide grin gave him a sinister air, his deep laugh chilling. "You should try them sometime. They make you manly." He paused, leaning towards her a bit. "And fresh is best. I've got a spare one in my pocket if you fancy it."

He got on her last nerve with his taunting. She bunched her hands into fists, wanting to punch this fucker's lights out. She glanced at Mike, and he nodded, putting gloves on from his pocket and patting the weirdo down. He removed a fluff-covered *thing* from Puffa's pocket.

Oh my God . . .

Mike walked away with Roland and Tory to the tree line, the testicle in his hand. Bethany followed, staring at the back of Puffa's head, wishing she could pummel it and get away with it, give him pain somehow, like he'd given to others. She strode on, determined this sick git would get the highest possible sentence. How many lives had he taken?

How many others had he ruined? And why, for Pete's sake? What reason could he give that would justify all this?

None.

They all trooped up the road towards the roundabout, and at the top, two police cars had arrived in their absence, officers directing traffic. The lorry on its side was a symbol — it had gone down just like Puffa would. A meat wagon appeared from the road Bethany and Tory had chased him on, parking behind Tory's police car. Mike led their man to it, and uniforms took over, grasping the tops of Puffa's arms. He grinned at her for a second or two, something red and fleshy between his front teeth, and she resisted running over there and slapping his cheek. They put him in the back and locked the doors.

Mike took a bag out of the car and dropped the *thing* in it.

Bethany stood there surveying the scene. The lorry, the traffic backing up, the curious stares of drivers coasting by, rerouted, their day disturbed by someone else's decisions. How far-reaching an individual's actions were, affecting not only the dead but the families and innocent members of the public. Tory, Mike, Bethany, Rob, and the officers here in attendance. They would all remember this, think about it, dream about it in the future. One man had touched so many, and all for the wrong reasons.

Ire burned inside her again, and she glanced at the grey sky with its just-as-angry-as-her clouds, wondering if Vinny was up there somewhere, watching her, rooting for her, cheering her on.

"I'm close to the end, Vin," she whispered and imagined him laughing his gentle laugh, which said: *You? At the end? Don't be daft.* She nodded, knowing damn well he was right. She'd keep doing this until retirement, but at the moment, with this roundabout disrupted, the fallout from Puffa's behaviour around her, she couldn't curl up into a ball and pretend it wasn't happening.

She took a deep breath. Straightened her shoulders.

"Fuck are you going to bring me down, you piece of shit," she muttered and answered her ringing phone.

"Call just came in," Rob said.

"What now?" She could scream she was that tired, that weary of people who caused so much grief.

"Dead body at the shopping centre."

Her whole body went cold. "What?"

"It's Thomas Volton, and his testicles are missing."

The world spun, the information circling inside her head, water around a drain. The blood on Puffa's face. Him saying fresh is best. The red between his teeth. The testicle in his pocket. He'd fucking *eaten* them *raw*?

"We're on our way," she said and cut the call. "Mike?"

He walked over from talking to Tory at the meat wagon. "You all right?" He cocked his head to study her, ever her protector, the man who cared for her because Vinny couldn't.

Fuck. She wanted to cry. Really cry.

"Volton's dead." She stared at him, telling him with her eyes what she couldn't say: *Help me with this one. Take some of the strain away.*

"I'm driving," he said. "And I'll take the lead."

Tears fell at that, and she followed him to her car, steeling herself for another corpse, another round of visiting the next of kin to give the devastating news of a pointless murder, one that only made sense to Puffa.

She sat in the passenger seat and cried all the way there, remembering how she felt finding out Vinny had died. If Volton had a wife, she'd be traumatised soon, her world forever changed. She'd join the widow club, that lonely institution that dished out so many emotions at once it was hard to see and think straight. Bethany wished with all her heart she could rescind her membership, turn the clock back, and be fully happy again.

The thing was, Death wasn't willing to hand it back to her. It was hers for life.

* * *

Thomas Volton rested on his back, the sight of his missing testicles grisly, the amount of blood in that area indicative that they had been cut off while he'd been alive. The pain of it . . . Christ.

Isabelle and Presley were already there, a tent erected over the body and surrounding area. Volton's face and mouth had blood on them, and it had leaked from behind him and pooled on the ground, viscous, darkening, a small piece of cardboard half submerged in it.

"You can move him now, Pres," Isabelle said once the photographer had finished. "I'm curious as to where that blood has come from — think he's been stabbed like Len?"

"Probably," Mike said. "Unless it's from a head wound."

"Too low for that." Presley got down on his knees and pushed Volton onto his side. "Oh. The weapon is still inside him."

Bethany craned her neck. Something metal stuck out of the skin around an inch. It was square ended. "What the hell *is* that?"

"No idea until I take it out." Presley sighed and put Volton on his back. He took his temperature gadget out. "But that'll have to wait until he's in the morgue, obviously. Now, this fella is still warm, so . . ." He used the probe. "Dead within the hour, maybe an hour and a half."

Bethany hadn't had a chance to talk to the lad who'd found the butcher yet, so she'd best get on with it. Fran was looking up the next of kin and had offered to go there with Leona and break the news. Bethany had given them the go-ahead. She'd had enough for today, and it didn't hurt to delegate sometimes. Didn't hurt to admit that no matter how much she wanted to do it all, be in total control, she couldn't. A step back would do wonders at the minute anyway. Her emotions were all over the place.

"Let's go into the shop then," she said.

Mike ambled along beside her. "Want me to chat to the kid?"

"If you wouldn't mind. I'm feeling a bit prickly."

They entered the building and walked to the meat-cutting area where the spotty bloke she'd spoken to before sat on an upturned crate, bending over with his head in his hands. Another employee stood by him, looking awkward, and he gave a tentative smile.

"Hi, DS Mike Wilkins and DI Bethany Smith," Mike said.

The body-finder sat upright and stared at them with glassy red eyes. "Oh God, it was that bloke we talked about, wasn't it?"

"We assume so," Mike said.

"What if he comes back?"

"Don't worry, he's been arrested. What's your name?"

"Wayne Norton." He scrubbed a hand over his acne-riddled cheek.

"What happened?" Mike asked.

"We were putting the delivery away while Mr Volton swept the yard — there were some bits of packaging that came out of the lorry, got everywhere. Anyway, we were in the meat storage fridge, and I heard a shout, and I said to Zach" — he pointed at the other lad — "'What was that?' We didn't hear nothing after, so I thought I must have imagined it. Then I got a horrible feeling so went to check if Mr Volton was all right. He was on the ground in the yard, blood all over the place, and this car was driving away. Green, couldn't see what sort it was. So I ran back in and told Zach, and he went out to the yard with me. Mr Volton wasn't moving and . . ." He heaved, bending over again.

"If you'd like to continue, Zach," Mike said.

Zach wrung his hands. "Um, err, we left him there and came inside to ring the police. I feel right bad about that, but I was scared, and Mr Volton looked dead. He was staring and shit." The last part came out as a mumble. "Then we waited here, and a policewoman came in, blood on her glove."

Nicola Eccles had checked for signs of life and found none.

"Right." Mike cleared his throat. "So neither of you touched him?"

Zach shook his head. "No way. We didn't even go near him. I saw the blood, saw him dead, and didn't want to be out there anymore."

"Wayne, did you get to see the driver?"

Wayne lifted his head. "No. The car was too far away, and it was the back of it, so . . ." He shrugged. "Sorry."

"That's all right." Mike wrote on his pad. "I saw a camera on the back of the building. Are the monitors in here or in the main office?"

"The main office," Zach said.

"We'll go through the shop in a second." Mike put his pad away.

"We got Simon to close it — he's the other assistant." Wayne rubbed his forehead. "Thought it best."

"Yes, you did the right thing." Mike smiled. "We'll be back in a sec."

Outside, they took off their protectives and handed them to Nicola, who put them in an evidence bag. Bethany followed Mike inside, and Wayne led the way through the shop and opened the front door.

"We'll be back soon," Mike said.

Side by side, they walked past Sandra and her balloon stall, then to the rear of the precinct to the lift, going up to the CCTV floor.

"You okay?" Mike asked.

She nodded. "Just . . . just tired of all this sort of thing. The death."

The lift doors opened, and they stepped out, showing their ID to the same receptionist they'd encountered last time. She pressed a button on her phone, and the black-haired fella poked his head out of the CCTV room doorway.

"Oh, hello," he said. "Can I help you?"

Mike nodded. "We need to look at some footage."

Black Hair waved them inside, where Blond was scoffing a bap containing egg, if the smell was anything to go by. Either that or one of them had a bad stomach. Bethany held back a retch at the thought and stared at the monitors and little TVs. All of them showed inside the precinct.

"Do you not check the perimeter cameras at all during the day?" Mike asked.

Black Hair shook his head. "Only at the jewellers when they have a delivery. Someone tried to rob it a few weeks ago like they did at the one in the market square. The lorry, I mean."

"Right." Bethany glanced at Mike.

"We need to see behind Volton's, going back two hours," he said.

Blond dumped his stinky sandwich on the desk and clicked his mouse. A piece of egg yolk fell out. The current view of the yard came on the screen in front of him. "Oh, fuck me . . ."

Black Hair walked closer and peered. "Shitting hell!"

The camera was trained on the yard and the road ahead. The tent looked odd beside the large wheelie bins, and Nicola Eccles paced at the entrance, getting soaked, the poor sod.

"That's why we need the previous footage," Mike said.

Blond got to work rewinding it, then set it to play on fast-forward until Bethany spotted the Fiat parking.

"Stop there and play at slow fast-forward, please." Her heart thudded dully.

While she couldn't see Puffa's features from that distance, she made out someone sitting in the driver's seat, facing the back of the shop. A minute or so passed, and he was doing something, then he got out and walked to the yard. Closer now, closer still. A poncho, a beanie hat, and what the fuck was that on his face? He glanced up at the camera. The shitbag *knew* it was there and didn't care. A white piece of paper, or perhaps a sticker with red lips on it, covered his mouth. Her stomach rolled with the weirdness of it.

He raised his arm, a weapon in his hand, and dug it into the top of Volton's back. She watched the rest with trembling legs, and once it was over, Black Hair and Blond shaking, Mike asking for a copy of the footage, Bethany walked out.

Watching someone get murdered wasn't ideal, and the image of it wouldn't leave her head. She rested a hand on the wall, the secretary looking at her funny, and closed her eyes.

Mike joined her and steered her into the lift. It sank with a gut-lurching jolt.

"I've told them to get counselling if they feel they need it," he said. "The pair of them are shaken up and upset that they didn't get to stop what happened. Guilt, even when you couldn't have done anything different, is a right wanker."

She nodded, staring at her reflection in the steel doors. She was a mess. Tired. Gaunt. Not like herself. Or not like she remembered anyway. When had that happened? When had she become so un-Bethany?

She'd put in for some time off after this. Maybe Mike would go with her to Spain or something.

"Fancy a package holiday?" she said, sounding unexcited.

"Can do."

"I need . . . a rest."

"Yep."

"Why didn't you tell me I'm getting to look old?"

"Why didn't you tell me I am?" He gazed at her in the reflection. He was haggard, too.

She shrugged. "Didn't want to hurt your feelings."

"Same here."

They laughed quietly.

"So now we try to find out why he did this," she said. "Did you see that thing he had over his mouth? It didn't disguise him at all. I'd know those eyes anywhere."

"He's off his rocker. I doubt we'll get to talk to him for long before we realise he's got mental issues, then we'll have to stop, get him assessed, and you can bet there'll be no chatting to him then because I'm telling you, he's not right in the head."

"I know."

They returned to the yard, sliding booties on, and Mike handed the footage on a stick over to a SOCO. Bethany dipped her head in the tent to tell Isabelle and Presley they were going back to the station, then they got in the car. Mike took to the wheel, and she rested her head back, closing her eyes, only to spring them open at the ringing of her phone.

Tory's name was on the screen.

Bethany put it on speaker. "Yep."

"You might want to come to the lorry."

"Why?"

"There are bodies in the back in various stages of decomposition."

"What?" Bethany sat straighter.

"And he must have lived in there. He's got a kitchen, loo, shower, bed, the Fiat, although it's all a bloody mess because of the lorry being on its side."

Bethany sighed. "Christ Almighty."

"We've closed the roundabout. There's too much evidence to risk cars going past in the lane beside the lorry."

"Good call. Okay, I'll let Isabelle know. Be with you soon." She swiped the screen and let her phone fall onto her lap. "Mike, this just keeps getting worse."

"What's happened?"

"There are bodies in the lorry."

"Jesus."

She called Isabelle, and they drove to the roundabout.

Would today ever end?

CHAPTER NINETEEN

Roland sat in a holding cell and leant over to lick the wall. It was better than nothing, and although it didn't taste of Mummy, he pretended it did. He thought of them all in the turned-over lorry, how they might have come off their hooks and scattered once it had hit the road. What were they thinking? Were they waiting for him to come and save them? Their downturned sticker mouths might have come off, and the police would wonder what they were, scattered just as much as the bodies.

A sudden need to see Jamaica Street gripped him, so he closed his eyes and walked through the house inside his head, seeing everything as it once was. The bed where Daddy had killed himself, the garden minus its stripes, the over-filled shed, the cedar tree, the sight of Mummy beneath it inside the plastic sheet, the neighbour poking his head over the fence and talking about spirits. Everything that was the house of horrors wavered in his mind, and then the meat fridge took over, all the naked, headless cows swinging, the pigs smiling with their hairy snouts upturned, and the lambs, baaing in his ears even though they were dead.

He wanted to put his face inside a cavity so badly he cried out from the need. He needed to sniff death. Breathe it in right down to his toes.

"Go and turn on the little light . . ."

"Find the order . . ."

Roland licked the wall harder, quicker, spit dribbling. Everything got tight below, straining.

"Let me make it grow . . ."

Wet filled his boxers, and he laughed a high titter.

He needed the other testicle.

Panicked, he shot up and went to the door, pounding on it. "Give it back to me," he shouted. "I need it. Give it back!"

Someone whacked the door from outside. "Be quiet in there, Didsbrough."

Roland pressed his back to the wall and sank down it to the floor. Tears filled his eyes. "Mummy, I want my mummy . . ."

* * *

"I want my mummy." Roland clutched Mrs Robertson's hand.

They stood at the cloakroom door, just the two of them. Mummy hadn't come to pick him up, and Roland had been peering across the playground for ages, waiting for her to appear.

"I know, love. Let's go back inside and ring her, shall we? Maybe she just got caught up with shopping or something."

"I'll stay here."

Mrs Robertson looked down at him. "Then I'll lock the door and you can watch for her from inside. You know you're not allowed past this doorway by yourself."

He nodded, and she reached up high to turn the knob, then walked off into the classroom. He imagined her going to reception to get their number and use the secretary's phone.

A kid kicked a ball across the playground, his jumper over his arm, the sleeve cuff trailing on the ground. Then he was through the gates and gone.

Mummy still wasn't there.

Tears stung.

He remembered last night, when Daddy was down on his knees in front of Roland, touching the maggot. Mummy had walked in, hair a mess from where she'd been asleep, and she'd stared, her eyes so wide.

"What the fuck are you doing, Lee?"

Her voice, sharp and abrasive, had hurt Roland's ears. And his heart, because she'd been there, she'd seen, and Mummy wasn't supposed to see, to know.

"He was crying in his sleep," Daddy had said. "I woke him up, and he said his winkie was sore."

"But you . . . you've got no clothes on. And you're . . . you have a . . . Get off him. Stop touching him like that, you bloody pervert."

Daddy had got up. "You need to fuck off. This is none of your business."

"It bloody well is. Come with me, Rollie. Come on, into my bed. Daddy can sleep in here." She'd taken Roland's hand and guided him to the doorway, then glared over her shoulder. "The police will want to know what the hell you were doing, Lee, and you'll have to explain yourself to them. I'll ring them right now. Don't you ever come near us again."

Daddy lunged at her, catching her on the temple with his fist, and she banged the other one on the doorframe, then slumped down to the carpet, her eyes closed.

"Mummy's sleeping right there," Daddy had said. "And I'll be in bed with you. We need to finish what we started. You go in, and I'll be along in a minute once I've sorted your mother. She can't sleep on the carpet, can she."

Roland struggled to make sense of what had happened.

He stared ahead now.

No Mummy.

Mrs Robertson bustled back into the cloakroom. "Your dad's just shutting the shop and will come to collect you. Mummy's . . . He doesn't know why Mummy hasn't come for you, but I'm sure everything will be okay."

Hot tears plopped down Roland's cheeks. Maybe she was at the police station. Maybe they'd come for Daddy later, then Roland and Mummy could live by themselves and be happy.

That was the last nice thought Roland ever had.

CHAPTER TWENTY

The back of the lorry was a shambles. Bethany and Mike stood at the opening and stared inside. A bed, the car, bodies, an old armchair, all of it had landed on top of a kitchen, a Portaloo, and a shower unit. The Fiat stood on its headlights closest to them. With the left side of the artic now being the floor, covered as it was with so many things, there wasn't enough space for them all to go in. Isabelle and a SOCO were in there, though, the SOCO cataloguing everything he could see by taking photos. Isabelle peered at the bodies draped over the top.

"He's had some of these for years," she called over. "And this one here . . . Absolutely gross. He's opened her up. I wouldn't be wrong in saying the innards found at the lay-by belong to her. The clothes will be Dave's or Len's. This is going to be one hell of a job sorting it out."

"We're talking days," Mike said.

It couldn't be helped. They'd keep the roundabout closed for however long it took.

"I've seen enough." Bethany stepped away, removed her gear, and handed it to Tory.

She got in the passenger seat of her car and waited for Mike, who drove them to the station in silence. Bethany wasn't complaining. She was drained, had no energy to speak, no words to explain how she was feeling. Spain was looking better by the minute.

In the incident room, she let Mike do the talking, and he filled Fran, Leona, and Tammy in. Bethany busied herself writing it all on the whiteboards, glad to be playing second fiddle for now. The girls chatted about the loose ends they'd been tying up, Fran getting Bethany's attention regarding the old woman who'd bought Puffa's house from him.

"She said he goes back there every year around the same time and just stands outside, staring in." Fran shivered. "The owner has to send him along his way, but he always comes back. He came a couple of times a week for about three months, then disappeared, only to return the following years."

"Did you find out when those three months were?" Mike asked.

"Yes, and it coincides with Roland's mother leaving."

Bethany's ears perked up.

Fran went on. "The story goes that she left them for another man, but some of the women who still live there from that time said it wasn't like her to just walk out and leave her son."

"Did they do anything about it? Tell the police?" Mike sighed.

"Well, no. They believed Lee, Roland's father, who told them she'd buggered off."

"Is there any record of her after she left?" Mike again.

"None whatsoever, either in her married or maiden names." Fran sniffed. "Dodgy if you ask me."

"Get hold of Thames Valley and inform them of this," Mike said.

"I'll do it," Tammy said and picked up her desk phone.

"The next thing is Roland's monetary footprint," Fran continued. "He only withdrew cash from a minimart at the end of Jamaica Street in Abingdon, and only ever during those three months. He withdrew one hundred and fifty each day, which resulted in around thirteen and a half thousand pounds. Do we assume he lived off that for the rest of the year until he returned to draw more out?"

Bethany turned to face the team. "How much bloody money has he got, for fuck's sake?"

"He sold his father's butcher's as a going concern and got a chunk from that, plus the sale of the house, which had no mortgage on it. He's basically been withdrawing interest, give or take a thousand." Fran consulted her pad. "As of today, he has eight hundred thousand, plus a few pounds and pence."

"I suppose if you're not paying rent or council tax, and all you need is food and petrol, you can get by nicely on thirteen K a year." Bethany glanced at the clock. "We need to go downstairs. His interview is in five minutes."

She congratulated her team on a job well done and told them to go home early. The paperwork and whatever could wait until tomorrow. Once she'd spoken to Puffa — she couldn't stop thinking of him as that in her head — she'd visit Kribbs, give him the lowdown, then go home, shower off the grunge of the day, and crawl into bed.

Outside Interview Room Two, Mike behind her, she took a deep breath and entered. Puffa sat at the table with his brief, a woman who appeared a little bored.

"My client wishes to tell his story," she said.

Bethany nodded and set up the tape. She took a seat beside Mike, and with Glen Underby standing guard by the door, she stared at the accused.

"Roland, I'd like you to tell me why you did this."

He glared with those bulging eyes of his. "Ask Daddy why he wanted the maggot."

She gritted her teeth. He was going to fuck her about, make her beg for information. Well, she couldn't be bothered. With the CCTV footage of him killing Volton, not to mention that testicle from his pocket, it didn't much matter whether he divulged anything or not. They had solid evidence, even if it was only for Volton at the moment, but having Puffa's DNA now, they could hopefully match it to something left at Dave's and Len's scenes, Angela's and Julieanne's graves, plus at Yasmin's house.

"I can't ask your father about the maggot because he's dead," she said. "Killed himself, by all accounts."

"Nah, I did it." He smirked.

She jolted more upright. "Did you kill your mother as well?"

"Nope, Daddy did that one."

He'd said it so casually it gave her chills.

"Why did he kill her?"

"I don't fucking know, do I? All I know is she took me to school one day then wasn't there when I came out. Daddy said she'd gone off with a new bloke because she didn't love us." His eyes glassed over, as if he'd gone inside his head to watch a memory. "She was going to tell on him. Tell you lot what he'd been doing to the maggot."

"What *is* the maggot?"

"What do you think?"

"I don't know, that's why I asked." Irritation gripped her. "I'm not into asking questions for the fun of it. Please answer me."

"Have you ever licked the inside of a cow?" He wiped imaginary mess off the table.

"No."

"What about a human? Mummy Julieanne tasted nice."

Was hers the body with the innards missing? She thought about the messages left on the animals in marker pen. "What's this about stripes?"

"Daddy likes them."

"Why?"

"Means he's done well."

Eh? "Why did you put a pen up a pig's nose?"

"To get it back for me having to lick it."

Pardon? "Can you elaborate on that?"

He told her a revolting story about mowing the grass, and if he didn't get stripes, he had to go inside the meat locker and do disgusting things to the animals. When he got to the part about the cow cavity and standing inside it, she retched, knowing damn well he'd done the same to poor Julieanne.

"Scary fuckers, dead animals," he said. "But the other cows, they didn't scare me."

"What other cows?"

"The mummies."

"Do you mean the ladies you dug up?"

"Yeah, them. Mummy's in Jamaica Street. Under the cedar tree. I found her there one day. That's when the spirit got me, made me do all this." He paused. "Have you ever had fat in your hair?"

What the fuck he was on about, she didn't know, but he was testing her patience, keep swinging from one thing to another. "Can't say I have, no."

"That's why I shave my head. Can't be doing with getting fat and blood on my hair if I rub steaks on it."

"Excuse me?"

"I buy a steak every day, wipe it over my head and face. Raw. So when the blood dries, it stinks. It's comforting."

She'd say a bath or being on the sofa under a fluffy blanket was comforting, not messing about with meat. "Why is it a comfort?"

"It isn't, it's terrifying. Reminds me of the cows in the locker."

"Then why do it?"

"I don't know." He drummed his fingers on the table. "I hate the smell of the mint from the shanks, but I still put it all over my face, and I eat the meat raw, lick the bones. Eat and lick Mummy."

She couldn't fathom why, if he hated it, he did it anyway. How could it be hateful and comforting at the same time? "Why did you remove the butchers' testicles?"

"To be manly. Daddy said if you eat them, you stop being a wimp. And I had to get rid of the spirit's laugh."

"The spirit's laugh?"

"Yeah, it's all high. Daddy didn't like it."

She needed to get back on track. "How many butchers have you killed?"

"Forgotten."

"How many bodies have you dug up?"

"Dunno."

"Why did you kill Yasmin Lynch?"

He narrowed his eyes at her. "Fucking bitch. She was my sister and stole my mum."

Bethany frowned. "If your mum died when you were little . . ."

"She didn't die, she left us."

"But you said—"

"She ran off with another man and had Yasmin, loved her instead of me. She probably had a nice daddy."

"Yasmin's father is deceased."

"I know, because *my* daddy's deceased." He may as well have added *duh*.

He wasn't making any sense.

"D'you know, I've had enough of this, Roland. I'm going to put in for you to have a mental health assessment. It's clear to me you're not fit to be interviewed at this present time. I feel you have unresolved issues that are detrimental to this interview, and us continuing will serve no purpose other than to distress you, me, and everyone else in the room. Interview suspended at . . ."

She left quickly, images of a kid in a meat locker chasing her down the hallway. She burst out into the reception area, and Rob looked up from behind the front desk.

"You all right?"

"No. Please get Roland assessed. I need to go home. Tell Mike I'm waiting in the car." She walked out so she didn't have to explain herself. If she had to remain in that station for one more second, she'd either cry or scream. Frustration at not getting the full story was bothering her, but how could she get it from someone as deranged as him?

She flung herself into the passenger seat and, not for the first time, asked how she could put herself through this time and time again, hating killers throughout the investigation then feeling sorry for them once they told her parts of their past. It took a toll, those seesawing emotions, and she stared through a rain-drizzled windscreen and actually considered talking to someone about it.

She sent Kribbs a message, saying she'd brief him in the morning, then switched her phone off. If it chirped at her again today, she'd throw the bloody thing.

Mike got in about twenty minutes later and immediately took her hand, giving it a squeeze. "I've heard Costa Dorada is nice."

"What?"

"For a holiday."

Her brain caught up. "Ah, yes."

"Fancy booking it over dinner?"

She rested her head back. "How? We need to put in for the time off."

"I've just seen Kribbs. Mentioned we wanted to go away. He reckons in two weeks' time is fine. We'll get it cheaper for a late booking an' all. Silver lining to everything."

She stared across at him. He seemed so tired. And he wanted to book it tonight. Bang went her idea of going to bed early.

"I need it as much as you," he said. "Besides, imagine what sort of haunting Vinny will give me if I don't make sure you look after yourself. Sorry, but he had a warped sense of humour, and I can just imagine him flipping all my picture frames over and moving stuff."

She smiled. "Yeah, he'd do that."

"So there's this place we can stay at called SunClub Salou."

"When did you get time to look?"

He flushed. "Took my phone in the loo just now."

"TMI, matey."

"So?"

She nodded. "Yeah, anything's got to be better than this shitty weather."

"Brilliant. Get a move on then. There's a takeaway to order at your place."

She poked his ribs as he started the engine. "Costa Dorada, eh? Who'd have thought it."

"It'll be magic, just you wait and see."

He drove to her home, and she thought a bit of magic was just what she needed. A beach, cocktails, the warm sun on her face.

Suddenly, life didn't seem so dire after all.

THE END

THE JOFFE BOOKS STORY

We began in 2014 when Jasper agreed to publish his mum's much-rejected romance novel and it became a bestseller.

Since then we've grown into the largest independent publisher in the UK. We're extremely proud to publish some of the very best writers in the world, including Joy Ellis, Faith Martin, Caro Ramsay, Helen Forrester, Simon Brett and Robert Goddard. Everyone at Joffe Books loves reading and we never forget that it all begins with the magic of an author telling a story.

We are proud to publish talented first-time authors, as well as established writers whose books we love introducing to a new generation of readers.

We have been shortlisted for Independent Publisher of the Year at the British Book Awards three times, in 2020, 2021 and 2022, and for the Diversity and Inclusivity Award at the Independent Publishing Awards in 2022.

We built this company with your help, and we love to hear from you, so please email us about absolutely anything bookish at: feedback@joffebooks.com.

If you want to receive free books every Friday and hear about all our new releases, join our mailing list: www.joffebooks.com/contact

And when you tell your friends about us, just remember: it's pronounced Joffe as in coffee or toffee!

ALSO BY EMMY ELLIS

DI BETHANY SMITH
Book 1: THE COLD CALL KILLER
Book 2: THE CREEPY-CRAWLY KILLER
Book 3: THE SCREWDRIVER KILLER
Book 4: THE SCORCHED SKIN KILLER
Book 5: THE STREET PARTY KILLER
Book 6: THE CANDY CANE KILLER
Book 6.5: THE SECRET SANTA KILLER
Book 7: THE MEAT HOOK KILLER

DETECTIVE CAROL WREN MYSTERIES
Book 1: SPITE YOUR FACE
Book 2: HOLD YOUR BREATH
Book 3: GUILT BURNS HOLES
Book 4: BEST SERVED COLD
Book 5: BLOOD RUNS DEEP

Printed in Dunstable, United Kingdom

64598797R00112